Snow

David Rappaport

Snow

Crown-Liquid Books

Published by Crown-Liquid Books, 2000

Crown-Liquid Books
P.O. Box 722601
San Diego CA, 92172-2601
www.crown-liquid.com

ISBN: 0-9679780-0-9

Library of Congress Catalog Card Number: 00-191387

Printed in the United States of America

Snow

1

How can I explain? How can one man inoculate another with the blue cloud of his experience? In another time the reader will receive a course of injections: a series of novels that combine to make pictures in his blood. Maybe then he will see the colors and the dancing girls. Maybe then he will know what it has been like, what the word "trouble" really means.

It was in the late evening on a Thursday not so long ago when I first saw her. I say this but, as with a recurring dream, it seems fundamentally incorrect to talk of, "the first time." They say that dreams are the blueprints of life; and what we call "déjà vu" is the brush of events against the contours of fate.

And it seems to me now I had premonitions. That I had seen her before she was there. There was some... animism, some intuition – altered, threaded through small happenings and things. Yes, there were allegories of her but I could not see them. They were hard to understand.

Well I was seated in my office, watching the light fade through the maroon liquor of pony glasses, enjoying the enforced leisure of prisoners and useless men. I was dressed in blue, with a shirt of canary yellow, with cordovan brogues, a cream display handkerchief patterned in burnt sienna with the insignia of a hotel where I once had worked. I had my feet up on the desk.

It had been a spell of wet weather and beyond my shoes the sky was deep ultramarine, dimly fluorescent and rhythmic as a gas is rhythmic, reverberating in the hills. It was the kind of weather when everything reaches down inside, in complexes of memory and emotion; somebody call it love. And the rain came on from split blue sacks of grain, a woman crying over the damned town, mere and translucent, on some opera jag after all the long time.

This is a tendency that can be called hardboiled – a shadow full of women and cars which filters like code through the pebbled windows, as through a gramophone, a radiator, some instrument. Me I had a telephone, a filing cabinet full of everything that fades. There hadn't been any calls in a thousand years.

Sometimes a woman comes, a long brunette wearing a brown wool coat the color of coffee, a green silk blouse and stockings, red leather pumps with stiletto heels. She stands for a moment in the doorway flickering and then she is not there.

And there must be some other name, for searching, for this life. A little trouble; but not enough. There'd been a certificate on the wall and now there was the yellow square where it had been, a nail hole, the rust... There were photographs on the walls, in front of the air ducts: blown-up images of mountains draped over in telephone poles and wooden fences chalked full with pictures of smiling men till you didn't hardly see them in the figments.

The walls were blue and green and silent as I sat smoking in the approaching darkness, in the long gas between day and night. Yeah, business had been slow but not for lack of advertising. I had a televised blue image of my business card on a closed circuit TV. My words crept through the city inside a pneumatic tube. So there was nothing to do now but wait in here, in the blurred days. I tapped a thick, white cigarette like a metronome on my wristwatch, struck a match on the beaten clock.

The ember glowed deep violet in the afternoon and it was the color and the slowness that made me remember: these... moments, changing... imperceptibly. Their forms remained, crept upon only by a migration of souls.

But anyway I remembered... "Summertime" on the juke box; the drone of dead words... Rat-tat-tat-tat-tat-tat-tat. "Over here, Sarge, this one's hit bad!" I fell with teeth to the earth. There were hands. The viaticum of booze – flicker of old metal to my lips, like some silent picture. Sons of the Desert just as I was going down memory lane.

It was like a room at evening: people rumoring in the hollow, wooden spaces; me withdrawing with the heavy sense of forgotten words. In dreams of drunkenness I made my way, finding so colorless my old uniform. There was nothing for me here.

And yet I remained. Something remained, hung around. And then it was a cavalcade of hospital wagons, a white, bandaged world; a winter more subdued than the ashen sky, the silver weather that crept like a needle. How he used to come in!

My cousin and I had joined up together, laughing, whooping, clapping each other on the back and saying,

"Soldier." The dark, noble uniforms; the echo and sudden fascination of place names in newspapers; the prospect of trains and ships. White sun glinted on the brass of the recruitment band, played tricks on our eyes.

He died in yellow dust, in the summer of that awful year, so grim and like a stone age now.

I got out with a head full of gas and a purple heart; a letter from the President and some green writing in my arm that still said, "Sarah," under small scales the years had grown.

The red iron rooftops, the white clouds, blue eyes and corn silk hair, the one sweetheart still waiting for me, with my Boy's Life comics and my drums.

When the plane took off, I could see our town. I could see our house. As I watched it got smaller. And I knew that she was going there. Maybe she was there already, sitting round the coffee table in the bright morning, with my parents, my dog, like dolls. That was too much.

You know, I wanted to write. But I always imagined my letters shrinking, until she could read them in her tiny hands. I was... changed. Too altered now to go home; for "home" to be anything but a word spoken in barrooms, lost in the jostle of elbows, the blue and the gray.

So I settled down in a one-room off Fountain, started skipping rope and working out on the bag. I didn't know if it was a convalescence or to get the rest of my brains beaten out. But I had to do these things, a guy like me.

They called me, "Soldier Boy." And again I began my slow romance of bandages, like the moth to the flame. Like the traveler returning in darkness to empty rooms. These days remember bells in the sound of the rain. "Get up, Johnny! Get up off the floor!" And I was going to. When I got around to it. There was just too much time.

So now by degrees the day goes by, moving beyond pale curtains. The cars glitter like garnet and work in the streets. I sit with my heels in the drawer, obscure. That was me in there. A guy with an office and a business card full of nothing. A guy that gestures and hopes and needs the work that comes drifting. You don't see much in this business but the inside of a glass. You don't hear much unless it's maybe something that could be the sound of wind on the desert and slow changes of the flesh. I try to read. I can no longer read. The books are closed, un-talking flesh.

And when it's really night, when the white chicken smell of Los Angeles wafts down the boulevard and the spindly black leaves of the palm trees wave their hands, well then I'm on the streets again.

I left the building with a late edition, walked out anonymous like a man washed in crowds. I smoked cigarettes and walked by windows, tightened my faded overcoat in the reflecting brass glimmer of hotels.

I went out, past the drugstore and the shapeless diner, past the pawn shop and green eyes in rows of TVs blinked and watched me go, with a single consciousness. They were replaced by umbrellas and then by dark girls with the look of clouds and bad dreams. I thought about going into the diner. I'd have some coffee. Sit and stare awhile, sifting through the blankness that used to be alive. Maybe I'd take in a movie or take a drive, the night sky reflecting in the window glass.

There must be something, somewhere. Something more than this. I was searching someone's rooms once, a writer. An insurance job and I was supposed to find some dirty pictures; and I took a very long time, long enough to read at the bottom of a drawer, long enough to know. That a certain hour of the evening always lived in pale yellow light, in the clink of a spoon on a cup, the mute proximity of women. I pushed the starter, slid the blue Lincoln away from the curb.

I took the Ten on down toward the ocean, driving like a song over the long quiet road. Round, glaring head-lights floated like a city behind. And then, as if in a cellular realization, several cars almost identical to mine appeared around me in the fog. The car drove through sheets of ocean mist, shooting flashes against the haze. Sodium lamps grew like flowers in the grainy dark.

I got off at Fourth Street and took Pico west, turned onto a side street and rode it alongside Main, down south beyond Blue City. Blue City in those days was a banana republic with changes of government arrived in a beige tide of police radios and drugstore Scotch. The whole place was one big dope racket and a network of back rooms where a guy could really lose his head.

And I had a flame here once. And me I had the hunger. And something that kept on turning. I tell you she still was burning. What was she? I don't know.

But at night sometimes when the wind is full and the clouds glow soft and blonde all over like a circus on the bay... Yeah, well maybe then I'll drive down her street, drive by her house, take a look in the window, at the ghost of her.

I drove away from there, with just the short squeal of tires in the night as she was doing things that were unrecognizable in lit rooms. And when I had got far enough away, when I'd driven clean of the memories, I pulled over to the right of some disused interurban tracks and an auto-body yard. I threw the stick into park, cut the ignition with a tinkle of keys.

I reached under the seat and used a flash on the darkness, felt along under the foot carpet until I found the bag. I took out the bamboo cylinder and opened the newspaper bindle, peeling the paper away from the ebony tar. I rolled it in my fingers and touched it to the flame, once or twice till it was soft, pressed it to the pipe's small, blackened hole.

The pale fire danced and the black ball sizzled and grayed and I needled it through, lit it again. And as the car filled up with the sickly, reminiscent, foody smoke and the rain drummed on the canvas, blurring the lights in the windows yellow and opaque, my eyes began to see into a different world. Esoteric thoughts. The stakeout grown cold and empty. The sleep of sex in darkened rooms.

Again I had done my meditation. And again I had the time. Again I verged on indolence, I who was so resistant to reveries. It was all gravy for me now.

I sat there and listened to the rain. And after a while I could hear the sound of it. I could hear the clearness inside the rain. When I was young. When I was a boy I had a little terrier. And when I couldn't sleep I'd put my hand on her. And the sleep of the dog would flow into me, perfect. It was something like that.

And yet some kind of residue still danced in my brain. Many periods of my life came together, unveiled of whatever cloth the mind uses to conjure time. There were memories, very complex, of my childhood that seemed to emanate from the color of a plastic toy. I recalled that color with great nostalgia; and it was again before my eyes, behind my eyes. Imbued with the sense of philosophy. A philosophy of memory and sentiment that disclosed nothing. I saw how a man could become a slave to his past.

And I said to myself, "How long have I lived in

society? Have I been here always?" It seemed the lights and the gathered dresses, the ephemeral postcard loveliness had taken something from me, in warmth and solicitude, through the years of beige time. I had seen some mesmerism, these stories. And me I had the memories – a shadow in the doorway and a figure I'd never known. Was it? Had there been someone who used to visit in the shade of slats, bringing some gray communion through the night? You don't get that. I shut the car, made out across the sea of lots.

* * *

The boardwalk was dim and empty, rotting with a smell of sandalwood and oysters, the cloying ghost of the ocean's dark country beyond the circus lights and the Grand Hotel. I thumbed a cigarette and the flame was small against the sky. Rain showed in gray flecks along the cigarette paper.

The surf roared in white noise beyond the bike path and the yellow swings, beyond the palm trees painted white and the shut, gray lifeguard stations. Down on Main Street a lighted City bus slowly pulled away. Dark shapes moved along the blue arcades as through the lenses of binoculars.

I walked along the boardwalk, past old women pushing

shopping carts and men wrapped in black trash bags. I got to the café and through the windows I could see the rush of pink faces, the soft, lit-up merge of women removed by glass. The rain was letting up, though a drizzle still ran in green film down the canvas awning and in my hair, under my shirt collar, down my neck.

I went through the door and the air was full of voices, loud, damp and acrid with a stale, institutional breath. Cigarettes dwindled from idle fingers and there were talking, diverted smiles. The air circled in slow, green clouds over the standing lamps.

Music was playing and on the wall, on a narrow shelf, there was an album: the cover was a silhouetted blue image of a radio telescope. The music was foreign and loud. I walked over the strip of trodden gray carpet to the counter and the fluorescent-lighted, refrigerated dessert case.

The walls were lined with bookshelves. The place had high ceilings. There was a loft over the front door, littered with books, speakers, a fan, all covered with a sediment of gray dust. The alcoves by the windows were occupied by thin, unbalanced, round wooden tables and rickety chairs. On the walls, above and between the bookshelves, there were garish oils. There were black enamel coffee tables littered with magazines, ashtrays and club fliers: *2plus2 Fun Factory, Saturdays at the Strobe.* On the wall, at the entrance to the gold-painted bathroom corridor, there were cubbyholes like hotel mailboxes full of advertising postcards. There were green leather smoking chairs, reading lamps with orange glass shades.

The place was still filling up. In the doorway there were pasty teenagers in green mod jackets. A girl in a dark, rain-matted artificial fur touched irritably at her hair. I leaned over, keeping my foot in the line, and ashed my cigarette.

"Hello? Hell-uh-o?"

I turned around and smiled and the blonde behind the counter gave me a look like I was the punch line to an off-color shaggy dog story. She had heavily-penciled pale green eyes and protruding, smoke-yellowed teeth and horn-rimmed glasses that did not make her look intelligent. Her small breasts poked like baby bottles from beneath an undersize lavender athletic shirt with navy piping at the border of the neck and sleeves, bearing the number 88 in blue lettering. A sloppy purple beehive tumbled around her neck and shoulders in wisps. Her cheeks were gray and she wore red powder.

"What can I get for you?" she said.

"Just a coffee."

"Regular?"

"What?"

"Regular?"

"Uhhhh... Yeah, just ahhh... regular," I said, "... yeah."

She gave me the coffee in a big tea cup and said,

"Four twenny-eight." I paid her and dropped the change into a dented brass bucket with a picture of a girl on it and the words "Tips For Lulu; Support Counter Intelligence" written in purple felt pen. Behind her a stocky guy in greaser sideburns and dyed-black hair, wearing a lime-green bowling shirt and tattoos of dice and naked women yelled in accompaniment to the music, jerked the grounds holder out of the espresso machine and banged it on the counter. There was a sound of rushing steam.

I turned around and edged through the people standing there, got to the condiment stand, stirred cream and sugar into the coffee, walked past tables of people who seemed to be reading, some more people who seemed to be writing. I made my way slowly over to a vacant red armchair near the door.

I sat down and settled back deeply into the chair, reached forward with effort and made a place for my coffee among the magazines and ashtrays on the coffee table at my shins. The chair was in bad shape and I had to reach up to lay my elbows on the armrests and once I had set my coffee down it seemed very far away.

Music was still playing. The ambient music had given way to some low-energy techno and there were endlessly repeated rhythm patterns of tinny electronic sounds that sounded like fast Morse code. Over to my left, on a tall night table, a glass vase held a single red rose. Some small movement caught my attention and my eyes focused on the dark-haired girl beyond, sitting on the green velvet sofa, her cigarette hand resting on her knee.

Her hair was thick and very straight and black. She had smooth, olive skin. An oval face. She was not moving with the music but seemed to be intently listening. I don't know why I had that impression. Perhaps her head was moving slightly back and forth. Her eyes were black and vacant and had an eager, anticipatory quality. Her mouth was open and there was lipstick printed in crimson smudges around the white cigarette burned down to her knuckles. She wore a dress of navy cotton without sleeves and leather sandals that were stained dark with rain. Around her neck there was a strand of small white pearls.

My first impression was of familiarity. I thought I knew her, remembered her from somewhere. And then a different feeling came over me. A flicker of distant recollection, like this was something out of a movie, or something out of a dream I had once a long time ago, as if there had been...

For an instant what I was seeing had nothing to do with the place where I was, with the light and the people and the sound. There were thick trees in a dark wood and there was a girl in the wood, moving through the trees. She was running. I thought she was running toward me. The scene faded from my eyes and I shook myself and could not understand the connection.

I looked at the dark-haired girl. Her eyes were almond-shaped, with thick, almost Spanish eyebrows and heavy, sullen lids. Her skin was brown. Her eyes were remote. I thought maybe it was just the familiarity of dark-haired women.

And then it all faded, swept away. Whatever had stirred in me became still. I picked up a magazine from the table and opened it. A shower of perfume adver-tisements fell from the pages like moths.

2

I got home late, fading from the lights and the moving cars up in Hollywood. I put a match to a cigarette. My watch face glimmered amber in the oblique glass and it was nearly three.

I had a room in a brick chateau on Fountain Avenue: The Iordica. Down a hall there was the sound of water slapping and a high, tremulous male voice sang "My Wild

Irish Rose." There was a mutter of televisions in closed rooms.

The lobby was upholstered in hard red leather. There were mahogany chairs and benches. The walls were papered in yellow with a green design of thorns.

The apartment had stayed while I was gone. The same hobbled furniture stood on the same pale carpet, threw shadows like horses on the same wooden floor. A round mirror shone dimly on the far wall, reflecting: a fidelity of objects that persisted and did not breathe, lent a restful, unphilosophic nature at the close of day, an almost marital sojourn. The atmosphere reminded me of a time when I used to rise at dusk, making my way from night into night like a man walking between cars of a train, walking on his own shoes for fear of losing his step. And then I would try and set to work, in that sanctuary where my head was clear of everything but all the familiar ways. There was a noise outside that could have been the sound of the rain.

I dropped the keys and small change from my pockets into a black plastic ashtray I got as a token of appreciation from the phone company one year. I went into the kitchen, flipped on the circular fluorescent and it blinked and quavered over the sink. I opened the refrigerator door, leaning on it haggardly, staring hard at the rind of orange cheese half-wrapped in foil and the bottle of dark beer. I shut the refrigerator, opened the cupboard and looked at the cans.

I decided I wasn't in the mood for eating. I took down the bottle of Old Forester from on top of the refrigerator, got a highball glass off the shelf. I poured some booze into the glass, swilled it around and smelled it and then poured out some more. I went into the living room, sat on the couch, stared at the TV screen.

There was a show I was watching. Kind of dim but always seemed to be on. About this guy. Guy who sits in his apartment without a lot of development. A couch, a coffee table. Some credit card bills. Come to think of it I guess you could say he was a guy like me.

Behind the sofa there was a green leather reading chair with a lamp beside it with a cracked yellow-orange shade. The lamp stood on a spindly black library table that stood in the corner of the wall. There were green drapes half-drawn at the sliding door to the balcony, falling straight down to the carpet. There was a fish tank that stood against the half wall that separated the living room from the dinette. Beside it my camera stood on a gray metal tripod, the bellows cracked and silted with dust like a wind instrument no one remembered how to play. On the coffee table a flecked, clothbound photo journal lay face down on the glass. In it there were curling photos I had taken. There were pictures of women, railway platforms, hotel rooms, birds.

I clicked on the TV and the picture faded in on a Latin soap opera; white cowboys riding out across the scrubby ground, shrill pistols cracking and screaming horses; a woman in a black velvet evening dress swept an upturned hand, indicating with a quiet, glossy smile a whole array of implements you would no longer have to use. Numbers flashed at the bottom of the screen.

I struck a match and held it while it flared, put it to the pipe and began to pull slowly. The tar bubbled and hissed and became gray and I drew down steadily, a deep lungful of that thick, sweet, cloying smoke that is always somehow a little sad, like abandoned ambitions, like the dreams of a sick man. Opium has the smell of something else, something you can't quite put your finger on and once you have smelled it it is the oldest smell in the world.

Lying sideways on the couch I watched the blue TV shifting and figuring, the standing images washing over me and over the room, lulling my eyes purple in the changing twilight and my head was so full of stories.

But I didn't really watch the shows. There was just the blank spell in the late evening, when the day was finally shot somewhere in the television fluids and there was nothing more to do but sleep. Sleep and wake to another day. A day that seemed it could be different. When I would give up the smoke, sober up. When I was going to begin my masterpiece – only everything seemed so faded and out-of-focus these days.

I lay there on the couch, after The Honeymooners, watching Movies Till Dawn on channel 5. It was an old picture and there was a girl in it, with red lips, dark eyes and raven hair. Songbirds tugged at her like a window. She mouthed some tender aria. Her skin moved like china on the old film.

And it was coming to me now: behind the TV, through the pictures and dim shows. I seemed to see, seemed to hear... chirping, like birds in a dark wood. They were talking to me now. And if I could only get the gist of it, get closer, get...

I started awake like I had caught myself falling. In the bedroom there was the last sound of the telephone and the clack and whir of the machine. Voice spoke in the darkness and said my name; then slipped away and there was nothing in the room. The sheer inner curtain caught the lights of the street, playing them back to me like a movie. I took a butt from the green ashtray and lit it again, sucked it alive. I got up unsteadily, went over to the sliding door.

I stood for a long while out on the balcony, looking out over the streets and the moving shades. A big black bird roused itself from one of the cornices with a noise of shaken umbrellas and flew languidly away.

On the boulevard a siren droned. I could see the circling red light fading, becoming small through the streets. The rain had stopped and only the damp hung in the air, soft and diffuse around small lights in the hills and under the yellow lamps hunched in the parking lots; the sleeping generations of darkened cars. Lightning flickered in the sky over the dark, blue Santa Monica hills. The signal turned on the boulevard and traffic started schooling back and forth.

I was reminded, distantly, of my own restlessness, of Sarah: "stay" in her eyes; my soul like wind in the porch branches. Something... grown. In me. Something that did not batten on all the long years. The strange hot time. "Think of me when you see the ships sailing, when you see the flags flapping on the strand. For all my heart's failing, I cannot say I will love you as well when I return."

In a matter of days, how quickly her outline began to fade. And she became like other women. Generic. She drifted from me, with nothing to keep her. Without past. Leaving nothing in her place. So long as a person lives our thoughts trail them about the world, gray and incomplete, curtains in a twilit room; only after death residing like water in a glass, gaining the flesh of ghosts.

Now I remembered Sarah with the clarity of things that are truly gone. Her form materialized, blonde, visiting, the windguest that cannot be trusted to remain.

She came around, like she did, moving vaguely, passing through my eyes occasionally but from the back, like a cartoon character, so that I could only see her in the half light.

I remembered... places. The sweetness of a gone woman lies in the breath of neighborhoods she brought you, that love unshutters briefly in their sacredness, that stay around in few moments of slowness amid the inexorable bureaucracy of the mind. She was beautiful. And yet her beauty belonged to the daytime and was bland. I got no mystery, no drug, no shady business in her eyes. I had to go searching, a guy like me.

And one night I found something but it wasn't there. It wasn't anything. Just the sorrow and the confusion and letting go in the white arms of another the one I used to love and call home.

As the days grew less and less I began to screw myself up to some kind of heroism, to find slogans. "Now begins the difficult part of love," I said – that is, loving when we were out of love.

And the silence came creeping like cars between us, somewhere in the vastness. It seemed every day things were moving out. She had wanted children. She talked about it the times we were still getting along, like an embroidery she was making, though now she had become whimsical. I hated children. They reminded me too much of men, with their violence and materialism. I seemed to lack the instinct of fatherhood. I had no love of miniature.

And there came a time when the vital element had departed; and yet still there was something; a kindness maybe, a desperation. We were like things in a box, eating up our air, using up our words till we had none left but the one, hard word we headed toward. "Goodbye." The last touch of fingers. The wasting thread. That fruit so bitter in the mouth.

I got a letter once, about a year ago. Her words were like hieroglyphs. I had already cried for Sarah, or the thought of her. That was when I still believed in tragedy. I have put down a cloth inside me. Tears are a veil through which nothing comes again.

I say, "tears," but that's wrong. My tears had gone a long time ago. What I had was deeper than tears. And not as much.

And yet tonight, maybe by some trick of the weather, I felt the occupancy of a race of feelings I had thought extinct. I felt the courage again and almost the desire to begin my philosophy; and I discovered memories of women, like a roll of film that had lain for so long in a camera's dream. They came out for me now, the spangles and the bathing beauties. They move around my inmate show.

"And what would you do if I told you I still loved you? What would you say?" Woman. She shimmers and she dances and you see her in the sky at night, though she tried with her cruelty to make you forget.

These lost ones, they were the talking girls who slip through one's fingers, who are discreet and constrained and cannot love enough. They cloak themselves and go. A law of repulsion governs their movements, drawing them back to those they love only approximately. There is something in the world that conquers true romance.

So they were destined not for me, fading – too easily becoming something glowing in the long night of retrospection, returning to their world of comforts and ordinary men.

And so I too had become ordinary – obscure, had become thin and transparent in the silent world. And the woman I had loved, for whom I would have died, one day I discovered she had died herself, somewhere inside, like the little gray mouse I kept in my shirt pocket, among the cigarette papers.

At one time or another I had longed for each of these women; thought perhaps I should have gone after her, found her in some foreign scene. I could have arranged to meet her as if by chance, walking down the same street in Belgium, sitting at the same café. "To add a bloom to our love." And if we met again... no. It could not have been without great mediocrity. The affair had played itself out, completely, though it seemed that cars and buildings had carried away the time.

But if I had my way; if hearts could influence the course of things. If love really did conquer anything at all. Love always was the poor man's truth. Poorer still since it was never built to last.

I was left with these remnants, these scraps that shift and move at the stir of some rare weather that with the passing years becomes rarer all the time.

Somewhere, it seemed, I had weakened. I had come under the thrall of the days. I had anesthetized my personality until it had changed and become unrecognizable somewhere in the long fade of heavy pleasures, somewhere in the gas. Somewhere in the drugs. A mind of any originality attempts to destroy itself, ruin itself in a dreamless world. There was a time I saw the familiarity – something that came to move in me and come alive. There was a time when I thought I would renounce this world of people, disclaim it and the life I was forced to call mine. I would devote myself and my real life would begin. At twenty I had the strength but not the quiet. And now I have the quiet but not the strength.

And as my life became slowly transformed from the big gift still coming of childhood and began to have the quality of a possession, more or less second-hand, I found, like a mute poet who feels but cannot express his fate, that somewhere the muse had left me and I was made for love alone; that only romance might turn me strength from weakness, work some bright alchemy from out the tired years.

There comes a time when the past, your own past, begins to seem the big mystery; when that something you could've sworn you saw never does flicker and turn gold; begins to change, fallen into darkened ways, wavering with a semblance of shadows in the depths of a woman's eyes.

That was how she'd gotten to me, the girl in the café, calling up strange longings, philosophical, almost artistic yearnings that might make me think I had been wrong, after all, to rate the value of life at so little, to allow my character to weaken, my feelings to wane. I had wasted so much time. Perhaps almost too much.

And soon the rain began again, gentle and surprising and soft as the cheers of a distant crowd. And then louder, like a man remembering his anger at the sound of his own voice. It rained blue, slick and splashing with a hiss of old leather, pelted with a vengeance down on the roofs, rushing and gurgling in the rain gutters. Sidewalks filled with the sound of it. Narrow boulevards with no names shone like rivers in the green hills.

The rain began again and like a man who somehow, against all his experience, still believes in the permanence of mental states; and who nowadays feels a tiredness and a skepticism in the presence of inspiration, who summons his inner life briefly and at odd intervals as a man might check his watch, I told myself I would think about it all tomorrow, when my head was clearer and I'd had some rest. Sleep was the vehicle that would take me. I went inside and rinsed the glass.

I got into bed and switched off the light. No dame flickered like a mannequin in the window. There was nothing here but me.

I smoked a few more pipes, lying on my side, leaning

over the licking yellow flame, feeling the need and then feeling it slip discreetly away, like a pimp into the night, returning at intervals to peer through the curtained window glass. And now slowly the pictures began to well and bloom. The long, long thoughts. Night's reddest flowers. Opium is a strange, contradictory drug.

I smoked and lay staring at the gray slats of the venetian blinds thrown slanting across the wall and the ceiling. And soon my thoughts began to coalesce, blend together, as in some epic of the silent age, full of clouds and horses, shifting in heavy colored slides. And I verged on the cities of sleep.

Outside rain drips from the aluminum gutter. The clock on the dresser abides, merging with the sound of the rain. Tik... tik... tik... tik...

And time must be a creature of desire, of will. Now the pale figures lay cheap and vacant on my eyes and the day, the month, the year were of little consequence. Time is still for the earth and stones. The present is fainter than the past.

And gradually my head grew dull and heavy on the pillow. And I thought I heard birds singing or the fitful, indistinct piping of children. There was blue-gray snow floating in my eyes like the luminous afterhaze of a TV screen. Then it all faded and changed and the figures turned and swirled around and like a desk calendar the months and ivory years rolled in yellow preamble to the

age of gears and clocks.
    And it was 1920.
    It was always 1920.
    And I was back in the dream again.

3

Or rather, I seemed to have been born into a series of dreams that lay one inside the other, that lay in folds on my person, joined with a long thread. And I didn't so much begin to dream as to find the world dissolving, coming away in pages and I was climbing down that thread into the small shantytowns of my mind.

Into a life I seemed always to have been living, only I

was forgetful. A life that had lain unremembered for so long.

What was it now? I never could remember very much. Only, it seemed I was a colonist, or a displaced nobleman or an officer after the war. And I was running from something. I didn't know what. Something told me that I would never know, that it was just one of those riddles that lie in the heart of a man, like a watch spring keeping him going, going with nothing but money and the long afternoons, the infinite leisure that seems the atmosphere of the past.

And it is Singapore, no... Shanghai. The place where nothing goes right. Somewhere in the far, far East. So far that it is almost the West again and everything has the pastel luminosity of early sixties celluloid and rice paper. Was it in the nature of opium that it bring on Chinese reveries? Can plants carry memories of their native land? I didn't know.

My dream was such that, at first, in the early stages, before it had descended into the ocean of sleep by the long stepping stones, I could observe it, study it, deceive myself that I was experiencing it in a detached, balanced intelligence and ask myself about the symbols that were presented to me, about the things that these called to mind.

At first it seemed I was walking in the woods on soft, dark earth. And I was searching for something with a flashlight. It occurred to me that the circular beam of the flashlight was like the translucent lid of a coffee can, as though in fact I were searching for something under a glowing lens fashioned from a coffee can lid. As though this would be the way to conduct such an investigation. But then the air of reason begins to disperse and, like a man who imagines he is looking at maps and timetables, succumbing slowly to the drifting cars, I put down this object I have been examining. I begin to stand up and then....

Then.

When was it?

Where was I now?

I came to this bar every afternoon, sitting at this cane table amid the waiters in white, moving in broad shoulders and the ease of habit long observed. The wind chime has lulled; the chaste barefoot girls are throwing water in pails along the dry clay floor.

And it is hot, so hot, watching the day go down in the insect world, glinting through the burlap and the gray shells, slow and yellow over the long water, the dark leaves waving in the waitress' eyes. They kept a table for me here. They must think me strange to be absorbed in the sunset and the evening glow, the boats like black Aladdin's shoes in the bay. But I was sad, you see, though I could never remember why. Maybe the bath girl had refused me credit; or some affecting picture I'd seen at the show. The strange Americana of horses, paint and feathers. Maybe the ghost of an Oriental nation flickered briefly over my uniform like film.

Yes, I think I was there, in that place. I was a... policeman; or a soldier. I had an image of the brown Army cloth. And these were the broken days, the wrong days. Deep in the blue heavy valleys of sadness, behind glass, before sound.

And maybe I was sad about nothing, full of that slow, ornate, subtle sadness that is nothing more than a voluptuous form of boredom, the virus of distance the astronauts brought back from the moon. My lips move like water lapping with the tide.

And didn't I read that the moon was like the East? I was sure I'd seen an article in National Geographic. That place where everyone must walk on stilts in the street. The people are small and inscrutable. At the back of every shop there is a little man who will supply your needs. Take care not to trust him!

And I too had become of the East. A Westerner subsumed in the Orient; most Eastern of all – a paradox. Everything is made of silk and the people's faces are tinged with the drifting and resignation. The long-faced dogs outside the hotel, playing cards all day.

And it seemed that I had become a real detective. And the small boy is here again, the small boy who comes around in the afternoon. He will take me to the place where they grow the flowers, he tells me. But to go there you need elephants, he tells me. And I tell him that I am poor.

And the dark-haired girl was in the dream too. She was dressed in white silk with blue stockings. She served me Scotch on the rocks from long porcelain spoons. What brand was it? I couldn't make it out. Perhaps Golden Monkey.

And I dreamt that I was hearing music. That the strains of a violin wended like strays. Sweet, cruel music. The saddest thing I'd ever heard. And she was there. Entwined. Caught in the unbreakable filaments of fate. Without music I would've been blind to the great sadness that surrounded us everywhere, in the ordinary things. Her eyes seemed to move from long ago.

And as she leaned over my table, the scent of her perfume settling like quiet understanding, I saw all at once, with inexplicable intuition, that she was a sainted nun, come like religion to my faithless years, like some sweet lounge singer spilling wine over the cigarettes and the mumbles, come to rescue me from the silence and the memories and the disused embraces; to tend and watch over me like the yellow moon.

I raised a hand, spoke to her; but it seemed she was perplexed. She smiled wanly and swayed. And then I heard the sirens. And I knew I couldn't stay. And then my lips were moving, recklessly, rapidly like a man who does not see his long loneliness. "But wait!" I whispered, feeling the words coming out of my mouth, "It's... it's all a frame!"

And then came the schism and the confusion. And now I heard what I was saying. I was trying to make her listen, telling her I would make it up to her; that it was not so bad to be dead. I reach to her but her body is cold and vacant. Her flesh grays to the touch.

* *

I awoke sweating in the darkness, got to my feet still reeling with the nausea of dreams. I went into the bathroom and leaned on the sink, stared at my face in the glass. It had a strange, shallow quality. The face a criminal might see. I cupped water to my mouth, washed down a yellow Valium and climbed back into bed.

I tossed and turned and then I pulled the covers down, beginning to masturbate languidly. The opium had deadened my sex.

I stroked myself, thinking of nothing. With great effort I summoned sex memories, girls I had known, making it at last, arching my back and desperately tensing as I remembered a girl with whom I had played in the woods behind our house, when I was very young.

* *

After a while I drifted off weakly into shallow, disturbed sleep.   And I dreamt that I was in my office.   It was around four o'clock in the afternoon.   In the customer's chair across from me there was a cop.

He was in plain clothes but he was cop to the bone. He wore a rough, gray-brown tweed blazer with sunglasses protruding from the handkerchief pocket, khaki trousers that were sharply creased from what I could see of the folds of his lap. The left side of his jacket hung more loosely than the other.   He was a big man, with gray eyes full of mirthless laughter, crew-cut salt-and-pepper hair, a gray-flecked mustache, a small chin.   There was still some baby fat on his cheeks and it made him look boyish, like a child that grew into a man just by getting bigger.   Something about him had the look of an old-time country salesman, the way a salesman would look if what he was selling people had to buy and yet he could take no special pleasure in his business.   He had the undead politician's look of all cops.

He made a sound that was half a grunt, half a sigh,

crossed his legs slowly and tortuously like a man who has got into the habit of moving as if he worked out the day before. Maybe he was running a marathon in the police Olympics. He smoked a dead cigar as coal-black and burned-out as his eyes. He played with my business card, worrying it under the thumbnail of his right hand, flexing the thumb back and forth. Finally he cleared his throat and said, "I gotta job for you shamus. A tail job. Missing person's job. It's concerning the dame."

"What dame," I said.

The cop fished with his hand in his inner right pocket, tossed a small photograph onto the desk. I twisted the brass switch knob of the green desk lamp.

The photo was bled-out. A snapshot. The kind of photograph with serrated white edges that had been in somebody's album. It had discolored bands that ran horizontally down it and there were yellowed triangles at the corners where it had been held in the photo album with Scotch tape. The photo was of two young people running in a field of long grass: a man and a woman. They were holding hands, delighted grins lighting up their faces. Their faces were in shadow and their backs were to the sun. The guy wore a floral print Hawaiian shirt of an indeterminate color. The woman wore a striped halter top and flowing rust slacks. The woman had pale skin and long dark hair, the hot black eyes even at that distance. She floated full of dazed euphoria, like a stripper on angel dust. The guy in the photograph I didn't know. I'd never seen him before.

The cop placed his hands out on the desktop, pressed them down. He looked at his nails. They became purple and then blue with the pressure and shone with the dimly reflected office. He bent his head toward me, pulled himself closer with the friction of his hands.

"Shamus, you think you can handle this job?"

4

Next afternoon was blue in the hills and the windows were already yellow in the gray office buildings – the day a fickle, wistful entity that wavered and had its freedom, gone away.

Had I dreamed? The red lights trickling; talk of violet in La Cienega; my face pale in the glass. Am I dreaming still?

An elbow; a cigarette wisping; some tousled hair; my eyes had the soft, crestfallen air of a man who rises late, for whom day and night are much the same – blended – who asks himself what time it is, reflects that it doesn't matter. For he inhabits the city, that is to say the world, but he is no more citizen than a flame is – a flame that frequented the long old ways, when we were sepia-toned.

I had awakened at intervals, closed my eyes, turned back into the dream. And now I could not remember it. It had sealed over at the end, healed, still somewhere moving its cargo but I couldn't sleep enough.

I looked out the window. The city moved like a TV picture and across the street the eucalyptus trees waved in the four-o'clock wind. Things called to me. Something outside of me. I had awakened, finally, to an image of red curtains; and the remnants of a melody stirring in my head. A memory of a dream of music.

And I thought the music was very good and I knew that I had written it. The room was dark now and I was left only with the sense of someone I had known. A counterpart. Not the girl in the café. It was another. Someone else that lent her skin. And her skin was white and pure as alabaster. I longed to touch it. She was forgiving and close as others can only be in dreams. Others who are oneself, for once. Who fade before the light awakes and spare us the pain and dull aberration of parting.

And because I had dreamt of her I made her my own, a component of myself that with waking fled into the world, into the clamor, making me say, "You can't leave! I've dreamt you!" though the plot fades and I become confused. Though I wake up with "you" on my lips like the flavor of ghosts. There it was again: that music; and the sense of living something a thousand times.

And it seemed certain I had known her, that there was a luster that could not exist out of time. But there was nothing in this life that supported it. This sense of years. A strange compression overtakes the days.

I raised my arm to smoke and the smoke curled up, illuminated in the faint, gray daylight. Pale green neon two stories high in the Reyes Building across the street said "Central" and buzzed in the darkness. I let down the shade. What there was left of the day wasn't worth looking out of a window at.

My brown hair was parted. There was blue file on my cheeks. My overcoat lived in a tough neighborhood and was the color of sand. I wrapped myself in the dull amber light that shone down in the hallway. I was wearing my dark blue suit, which gave me a vague, makeshift respectability in a variety of situations – hotel lobbies – where I was always slightly, but only slightly, out of place. A cream silk dress handkerchief was folded loosely in my breast pocket. I wore a shirt in a dark color, of a pattern no one remembers and my tie was printed silk and on it there was a picture of an Indian who didn't have any clothes on. I went out.

I drove the Lincoln up from the garage. Outside the strong, brown smell of Los Angeles greeted me, sharp on the evening air and down the hill the city purred with a hard, undulating purple and red-orange taillights flowed loosely in the streets. I drove east.

I drove up to Franklin and rode above Hollywood, up and down the small hills. I thought about going to the Olympic Auditorium and taking in a fight. But I didn't care to see more of those boys – all the new chin bums that waltz in the glare and get up slowly from the corners, looking androgynous and morose. The white towel fans, the sea of eyes, the cool, unmagnified crowd. There was nothing for me there.

I thought about eating in a discolored diner. Everything is faded. The water is colored in the glasses. The fat cook sits in front of the box and it flashes on him with soap commercials and pictures of money. The grill pops and sizzles like a crowd in a radio ballgame. You don't remember the faces. You don't remember the words.

I thought about going downtown to the cigarette crowds. It gets you all over in the light and the people and the sound. Maybe I'd go down to the Telegram Room, get my eyes affected with legs and mouth. There was beer in the place. And good safe chairs. They used to have a guy down there who played the piano standing up. But he was killed in an automobile accident. I drove east, down in the blue sweeping streets and the darkness lit cigarettes.

I got to Western and drove up the curve, continued on through Los Feliz; the park, the hills, the feel of sanitariums and green, wide, rolling lawns.

* * *

I sat in a broken kitchen chair, not smoking in the evening darkness, staring blindly out at the traffic and the clouds. Outside the steamed front windows people went by in vague smears. Old men played chess in an alcove by the window, the pieces standing like the pillars of a biblical town. In front of me on the table there was a glass half-full with red Italian soda.

I was in a café on Vermont where I liked to go sometimes in the afternoon. I would go there and it was like I was doing something. I'd sit smoking in an armchair by the window. Turn things over in my head.

Last night I had smoked too much. I had smoked like I could sicken the need. And now I felt the cold and the anxiety curling tighter and I could imagine vividly the drug giving up its familiar pleasure, like going home. It is monstrous to reject the familiar and I knew that, except by some providential accident, it was beyond my power. In this case there was no green plane to take me away.

This idle life has its peculiar sickness, its tides. Now was the time of great longing: a strained, homesick period when it seems the past can't have escaped. When it seems plausible to write letters.

In this frame of mind a man might telephone someone he hasn't seen in years. A strange telescoping filter operates on his perception of time. And the past will seem immediate to him. By a kind of mediumistic hallucination he will imagine himself capable of communicating with the dead.

They say that when one sense is taken away the others become sharper. What they don't tell you is that if a sense is taken away and then returned it becomes sharper too. The richness of this remembered life is a product of keen addict's loneliness. The loneliness of a man who belongs to another time. "Why am I thinking of you now?" I muttered, feeling some impulse to say the words, like a man who suddenly almost believes in prayer.

Some days I get the feeling if I went home I'd find all my old friends exactly as they were. They wouldn't have changed. And I could start all over again, right where I left off. And this time, would I do it right like I never did? It's like the old joke about the guy talking to his doctor.

"Doc, when the bandages come off, will I be able to

play?" "Ahh gee, that's swell cause I never could before."

The glass door swung open and the serving girl came in on a gust of air that was damp and gray and cool, flicking the first tinsel spatter of rain. She moved through the room almost in slow motion in the relaxed lounge music, her breasts slowly swaying and surging against the fabric of her blouse. Outside the clouds spread like watercolor beyond the jagged rooftops of the brick apartments.

The girl carried a black tub of saucers at her hip. She was a tall blonde with shoulder-length, brassy-yellow, slightly wavy hair. She wore a tight-fitting lime-green sweater and large opal stud earrings, dark red lipstick and tweed slacks. She was thin and her breasts were full and pressed against the fabric of her sweater. I called to her, asked her if I could get a refill on the soda.

* *

She came over with a fresh glass of soda, sat down, got out a cigarette package and lit a cigarette.

She reached out her left hand and thumbed a film of cold, gray sweat from my forehead. "You don't look so good."

"A private dick can show signs of dissipation," I said and leaned back to blow smoke over the purple room. I said, "I'll be okay, Angel. Just... Well I guess you could say I'm on a case." I took a smooth, brown wallet from an inner pocket of my overcoat, removed a pale, blue card and set it down. She picked it up from the table and looked at the writing there. I told her about dark-haired girls and memories and things that I didn't know. Somehow it seemed like I'd told this story a hundred times.

"So let me know if you find out anything," I called to her as she watched my overcoat flutter in the breeze. She stood in the doorway. And then she turned and walked back into the café and I could see through the window that she had taken away my glass and wiped the table clean and the doorway was dark and vacant and it was like I was never there.

I stumbled out into the drizzle of Vermont Avenue. The evening was cold with a dark blue wind blowing down from the Hollywood hills. I turned up the collar of my overcoat and walked along the shiny streets, under pepper trees tossing their leaves in the blue, darkening afternoon.

I went and had bourbon in a red bar on the corner that looked vaguely like a circus tent, came out into a night of rolling clouds; turning to black and the gray streets filled up with rain. Cars became slow and cold and deliberate.   Feeble yellow headlamps glittered in the splashing pavement.

I got to the car and didn't go home. I smoked a few pipes in the car, breaking off chips and taking down the smoke like food. And then I drove around town and the hours were like a carousel.

I drove through neighborhoods, like I used to. The city had come to inhabit me, so that I didn't see it anymore. As I moved through these neighborhoods it was like I was moving within myself.

I drove and the face of the girl floated up to me from out of the bare streets, out of the jovial silent smokers on the billboards on Sunset, the crowd emerging from Nude Nudes, the Singapore Airlines girl, looking at me with infinite sadness, as if I was an innocent man driving by on his way to a crash. I would look and the face would be hers. And then I would look again and I would see that I was wrong.

I drove aimlessly through the black streets, the neon signs. She came on to me in the faces of all the girls.

I drove on downtown, drove along Spring Street and the people world briefly transformed in the rain close to something living and human. The rain came down with the burnt copper smell of city, falling slow and yellow under the street lamps, showing up in white scratches in the headlights of cars hissing by.

I drove down and ate at a coffee shop on La Cienega,

had steak and eggs in my damp clothes.

I drove home on Fountain. A police siren wailed by me, brushing the draft and all. I went home and switched through stations, through magazines, played cards with myself. In that yellowness. I fixed a drink and lay on the sofa. Light flickered over me. A show about a detective. But it wasn't true to life. After awhile I pretended to sleep.

* *

The clock hands had moved and it was later when the phone rang. The moon droned softly in gray clouds. I lifted the receiver from its cradle. I spoke slowly, softly into the telephone. My voice was anonymous and remote: "Hello?"

"Johnny? Is that you?"

I said, "Yeah, it's me."

"Yeah, well... I got something for you. Some information."

"Yeah? Hold on a second." I went inside and got a paper and pencil and held it against the wall with the edge of my hand, held the phone in the crook of my shoulder. "Yeah? I'm ready... Yeah?...Yeah?"

I thanked her, told her I owed her one, hung up the phone. I went into the kitchen and made some coffee in the electric percolator. I combed my hair and washed my face. I simmered some marijuana in some olive oil on the stove, ate it with a piece of bread.

5

The windshield wipers squeaked over the smeared glass. I switched them off. The radio murmured inaudibly, just a yellow glow of numbers in the dashboard and the buzz of human sound. I drove up the coast, past Zuma, along ragged cliffs spending themselves in the sea. The sky was low and dark over the hills. But here the road was dry, blue with the empty evening, with only a few big drops of rain driven in rivulets by the wind.

"And my hands can touch the colors..." *The words came like a voice at my ear.* *I drove by fenced-in fields with a few bare trees moving slowly in the wind; a distant gray house with yellow windows. The sun was a cold gray flashlight behind the sea clouds. And with a clutch of anxiety, as though the scene had been replaced by another, almost invisible, less benign, that waved in the glass, I remembered... heavy red curtains, stone ceilings, the diffuse purple dark...* *"Yeah, hello? Anybody there?"*

I was standing in a wooden phone booth leaning against the green felt paper, with the black receiver purling in my ear, my foot against the door holding out the sound. It was in the ballroom of a cream hotel on the edge of MacArthur Park that had once been respectable, that was slowly going to pieces like chalk under the many bright days.

Through the window I could see the dancers moving before the condensed green light of the bar. My hand was stamped with an eclipsed sun: a dark circle with flames around it like flower petals. The colored light of projectors floated in garish film over the walls and the red heavy curtains by the stage. The thudding bass of the warm-up DJ was drowning out the phone.

I spoke again into the mouthpiece: "Hello?" I held the phone in the crook of my shoulder, with my face to the wall. I hunched over my briar pipe, thumbing a dry, gray plastic lighter. The flame caught, the muggle crept over me. And with the sense of gone timing I lost the thread of my thoughts.

I pocketed the pipe still warm and smoking with my thumb on the bowl. I hung up the phone, walked out into the disha disha disha of heavy scratching, clove cigarettes and the flower smell of Raid.

I walked over to the bar, toward silent KTLA news images going on the TV. It was an enormous room with high, vaulted ceilings. The walls were paneled in dark hardwood until about ten feet up and then they were quartz-gray marble that was smooth and veined. There were brass wall lamps standing out from the marble with shades of thick red-orange glass. Massive wrought iron chandeliers hung over the dance floor on chains. Out on the parquetry dancers moved in shades. It was a different room than the one I'd gone out of. The weed did that much. The weed in my stomach was starting to come on like mushrooms, a deep, vibrating, physical buzz.

Patterns and loop films flickered on the smooth, oyster-colored walls, shining from flickering projectors mounted over the EXIT signs: bathing beauties danced in silver lamé bikinis, pointed ray guns that looked like rocket ships; a row of South American Indians in feathered regalia floated continually to the left with the insistent, unvaried house groove, always in time.

I stood at the bar and smoked a cigarette looking out

over the floor. On stage there were consoles of dials, switches and meters. There were reel-to-reel tape recorders and green computer screens. Thick black high voltage cables wound down the stairs and out into the street to the gas generators.

The lights went out and people came away from the walls, drifting onto the dance floor and moving in a green sea of lighted cigarettes.

I trailed around the edge of the room, past a long-legged brunette in a low, scarlet dress and fishnet stockings, with a white cigarette tray slung from her neck on ribbon. Her face was illuminated in the light of a gooseneck pencil flash.

"Cigars? Cigarettes?"

Fingers of colored light began combing through the fog and vanishing. In sudden illumination men worked over the controls and heavy rhythms traveled the room. There were clouds of slow smoke, revolving and wisping as the gray specks of the mirror ball floated over the people and the walls.

I shouldered toward the center of the room. In the music there was a profusion of voices and a woman's voice wailing and a garish white searchlight swept over the fleeting hectic faces of the crowd.

I searched for a sign of the dark-haired girl and then the room was dark and quiet and a girl's voice said something that was unintelligible and repeated. The beat kicked in and the crowd moved in a mute, anonymous surge. Across the walls flashed pictures and star patterns and footage of solar flares and silhouettes of B-52s.

Blue and green lights passed over my eyes. I was moving and sweating and the people passed before me in a cloud of nauseous motion. The groove evolved to a closed, hypnotic loop, the samples and rhythm patterns repeated over and over. The crowd moved as a single entity, entranced.

Light flickered whitely over the unconscious dancers, and thin frames of strobe began flashing on the room. Suddenly, out of the corner of my eye, I saw her.

She was illuminated for moments in the strobe. I saw her dancing in changing frames. Her black hair was drawn back in plaits. I saw her lit up and going in gray stills like old kinescope photographs of running horses and walking men. I can't describe the way she moved. People don't move that way any more.

Clouds of smoke turned slowly overhead, shot through with grainy rings of blue and yellow laser, revolving and disintegrating. Gray motes swept the room in a continuous, unbroken feed.

On stage topless dancing girls with Xs of black electrical tape over their nipples gyrated in the blazing light, yelled, "Whooooooooo!" while club kids with rainbow afros and platform sneakers shot water pistols over the crowd.

The dark-haired girl was swaying, stamping, her eyes white, shaking her head. There was footage of blooms opening in red fullness, withering. She danced from foot to foot like an Indian brave. On the wall blue clouds boiled darkly over the land.

I tried to reach her, through the crowd. The people moved in a forest between us. The sound was deafening now. The air was thick with shapes.

I moved to her, through the people and the smoke. I took an elbow in the ribs and lost the ember of my cigarette. I got closer, closer...

For an instant I thought I saw her reaching out to me in the strobe, pale and silent and flickering like a heroine in an old film. I clutched at her. I saw her whirl, jerk away, disappear into the crowd.

The dance around me was feverish now. In the space where she had been I knelt down into the purple darkness. I picked up a trampled red matchbook, examined it by the flame of my cigarette lighter.

6

Next afternoon I woke up to the sound of leaf blowers, full of worthless fragmentary dreams. I tossed and turned, went back to sleep over and over, finally waking in the gray room mottled with sunlight, sitting up on the edge of the bed.

I went into the bathroom, splashed cold water in my face, walked out into the kitchen and put the coffee on the flame. I sat at the breakfast nook, rolled a cigarette from butts and ends and stuck it in my mouth.

It was one of those midtown afternoons where time seems to stand still. The moving gray shadow of leaves on the dinette wall merged with the disjointed sounds of traffic in the street below. I had taken a Valium the night before and right about now it was hitting me like a ton of bricks.

Over the boulevard the sky was clear and there were big dirty white clouds pluming up beyond the Pasadena hills like a nuclear explosion. The weather had gone hot and dry and scuzzy. The Santa-Ana winds had come. And there was a terrible dryness in the air, as if the desert had finally drifted in and done a repo job on the city. Everything had grown dead. The scrub in the hills was rust-colored and ready to burn.

The coffee bubbled out of the electric percolator. Some of the fuzz cleared from my mind. And I began to remember my dreams.

I drove the Lincoln down to Blue City, through the sullen, waving heat and the dark mirage pools that lay on the road like molten lead. I wore sunglasses dark as welder's goggles and they didn't cut the fantastic whiteness. I carried the striped pink matchbook cover in the vest pocket of my glen plaid suit.

I put the car on the third floor of the blue-tiled, four-story parking lot on Second Street, right across from the old, broken-down porno theater next to the youth hostel. The porno theater didn't even have a projector anymore, just a big-screen TV underneath the old screen with a core of die-hard perverts huddled around it. Behind the theater there was some walk-up office space and beyond that there was the beach.

I stopped for breakfast in a small restaurant on Santa Monica Boulevard – toast, coffee, some eggs. A blue-haired Filipino waitress came up and gave me a plastic-covered menu with black vinyl embroidery stitched around the edges. She wore high-heeled slippers of green translucent plastic with air bubbles inside like hand-blown glass. At the table in front of mine a Mexican cowboy sat and looked out of the window in a straw hat and a red Spanish shirt with an upside down horseshoe stitched on the back. The window was plate glass and flecked with yellow water deposits that were illuminated in the slanting sun.

I took the matchbook out and turned it over in my hands. I opened it and looked behind the cardboard stub that was all there was left of the matches. The matchbook was white and red, with thin, tapering, white, vertical stripes down the front and on top of this there was a valentine heart that threw out rays that extended beyond the edges of the card. The back of the matchbook was solid crimson. No information. I searched the match-book over a second time.

There was some fine black print at the bottom edge of the card. I got out the magnifying glass I carried on my keys. It read: Layton.

I went to the pay phone in the bathroom and pulled up the white pages and rested the plastic holder on the shelf. I leafed through the pages of the business listing. There were four Laytons in the Los Angeles County. One was a food broker, one was a maker of wigs. The remaining two were dubious as to occupation. One of these was "Layton Incorporated" with an address in Bell Gardens, the other was "Layton Co." in Manhattan Beach. I called Layton Incorporated first.

The line buzzed and then there was a hoarse man's voice that yelled over the sound of rushing machinery and said something unintelligible. In the background there was the sound of many people yelling excitedly and the grinding of trucks in low gear.

"Yes, hello?" The phone at Layton Co. was answered by a pleasant, middle-aged-sounding woman with an accent of the deep south who intoned all her statements as questions. She told me I had the wrong company. She said there was a Layton Paper in the Valley. She said maybe they could be the one.

I said it was worth a shot and thanked her and hung up with my finger on the lever. I dialed information in 818 and asked for Layton Paper and got the number of a Layton Paper on Lilac Canyon Road. I called and got no answer. I called information again and got the address. I decided to take a drive.

* * *

I drove on Sepulveda between the hills, down into the fading rippling yellowness of the San Fernadino Valley. It was hot, very hot, ten degrees hotter than in town. I took a right on Ventano Boulevard and drove east with the windows rolled up and the air conditioner on. It didn't help much except in the spaces when the car moved through the shade of buildings. I drove and wound along past boutiques and delis and dirty book stores, past a hot dog stand in a yellow box car.

It was a long way on Ventano to Lilac Canyon.

I got to the address I had written and the place was pretty run down, shut and gated; any sign of Layton Paper was gone.

It was a small, beige-colored, one-story office building across the street from a white stucco motel that had seen better days. On the second floor balcony of the motel there was a pregnant woman with dusty blonde hair sitting on a patio chair. On the ground floor some kids were playing in a broken brown corduroy easy-chair, throwing the yellowed stuffing and running around hitting each other with springs.

The place had bleached white gravel on the gently peaked roof and a faded plastic sign that said, "Color." The place seemed to have gone residential and there was a swimming pool that still had some water in it. That was covered with black plastic held in place around the perimeter with rocks of the same general type as the white roof gravel, only larger.

I turned my attention back to the office, cupped my hands to the glass and looked through the dusty window into the dimness inside. There were stacks of papers and office supplies and obscure machines. I had no way of knowing if they ever made matchbooks.

I took a billfold holding a phony badge out of my jacket pocket and crossed to the apartment building. I held it up to the woman on the balcony. She had blonde hair the color of wet straw, a gray complexion. She was wearing a pale blue house dress of thin denim. She was staring directly forward with an absent expression. The baby in her lap appeared to be asleep. I called up to her. I said, "Hi," and smiled engagingly and waved my arm. She didn't look at me. I said, "Uhh, excuse me, ma'am... ma'am?" I went over to one of the side stairways to the second floor balcony and began to climb up. "Ma'am I'm from the Bureau of...."

The woman with the baby got up suddenly and went into one of the rooms and closed the door behind her with a bang. The gray screen door pumped on its pneumatic closer and then it settled and then it was still. I turned around and walked back down.

I went over to the kids. There were five of them. Four were playing in the easy-chair. The fifth was sitting on the edge of the covered swimming pool, splashing his shoes in a shallow puddle of water that had pooled in the black plastic. I went over to him. I took out the matchbook. "You ever seen this before, kid?"

* * *

The sun was low as I drove back into the city. I took Lilac Canyon south over the hill, down into the city as it became Crescent Heights again. I didn't go home. I drove over to Fairfax and had dinner and took in a movie. I didn't remember the pictures.

7

Next afternoon I drove back out to the beach and parked the car in one of the diagonal metered spaces on Ocean Avenue. I walked along the narrow esplanade that runs along the bluffs.

There were palm trees and green cactus that lovers had carved their names in. Vagrants sat in the shade of the palm trees selling watercolors and pinwheel toys made out of old beer cans.

Gulls wheeled in the space over the Coast Highway and the lots of the pier. Out to the west at the ocean's horizon there was the thin, uneven purple band of Catalina Island. At the beach it was a mild afternoon. You would take it for spring or maybe late summer except for the grainy white light and the quiet forsakenness in the air that stands in for winter in LA. I lit a cigarette, smoked it looking out over the sea, crushed it out and started for the pier.

I walked down the ramp and onto the wooden boards of the pier. I walked past the carousel rotunda, past the shop devoted to plaster, the shooting galleries and the bumper cars. The sea sloughed restlessly with a noise of horses around the white posts.

I walked out toward the end of the pier. Gulls flew and squabbled in the air over the opaque, olive-drab water. There were flashing lights and whirring and buzzing sounds from the arcade. There was the rank smell of bait, old water and tar.

I found the small, blue palmist's shack at the end of the shops, next to a stand that sold lemonade that was run by a young black girl with her hair in tight braids. There was a hand-painted sign in brushed cursive that read "Madame Sapphire" and had a crude, flesh-colored painting of a pyramid. Under that were the words "The Unseen World." At the front of the shack there was a divided door that was shut, top and bottom. There was a lighted plastic buzzer beside the door and a sign below it which read "Ring Bell." I pressed the buzzer. After a minute the top section of the door swung open.

She was a middle-aged black woman in a thin, pink and yellow floral print dress. She was not old. But there was a strange deadness to her features. Her eyes were gray, opaque and steady like the eyes of a blind person but she was not blind. Her gray, fragile hair was braided carelessly and worn without style. Her movements were robotic and stylized like the movements of an invalid. She gave the impression of a librarian or a civil servant.

Before her on a ledge that extended inward from the lower half of the door there was a deck of cards spread out. Around her the doorway glowed with white bulbs.

"You have... questions," she said, as though guessing at a charade.

I said, "I'm looking for a girl. She dropped this." I pressed the matchbook forward across the narrow counter.

"Cost you twenty dollars." She took the matchbook and turned it over in her hands, rubbed it between her palms. She closed her eyes. For a long time she didn't say anything and after a while her breathing became slow and rhythmic. Her hands were in her lap. She began to chant to herself in a foreign language, saying the same words over and over. As she chanted she began to seem older and older. After a long while she opened her eyes and looked at me.

"I get the feeling of a woman in the past. Not this time. I.... I'm sorry. I cannot tell you anything more."

"But I don't..."

"Time is a chain," she said, pushing my twenty back across the counter.

I turned to walk away from there. As I walked away I thought I heard her mutter, "Seven." The words were distorted by the wind.

I went and bought a hot dog at a stand near the arcade, found a pay phone and went through the white pages.

There was a club in Culver City called the Seventh Vale.

8

The place was at the foot of the Culver hills, below olive-colored chaparral and rusted oil derricks moving un-focused in the heat-blurred air. There were remnants of street car tracks. Soaped windows in out-of-business stores. In peeling cigarette ads there were smiling black men holding trumpets.

I put up the canvas, parked in an unmetered space

parallel to the curb, in front of a sunlit link fence before a blue parking lot that lay in the shade of a red brick building that contained a Pakistani restaurant.

I got out of the car, walked back to the main street, whistling and jingling the change in my pockets.

It was one of the older buildings on the block. It used to be a 49¢ movie theater and you could see "49¢" lettered in fading purple on the curling sign. The name of the movie theater had bled out and was unintelligible under broken, colorless neon tubes. The marquee was ivory-colored in the late sun and just empty lines.

I took a long step toward the box office, over smooth, pink-flecked stone. Above a fluted plaster seashell and scrolls there was a small chrome grille. There was nothing inside the box office except a jagged piece of rough plywood right behind the grille. I stepped back into the sunlight and squinted for an address. It was the kind of place you could look for for hours and not find it while some bum in the alley is falling in through the front door.

I pushed gently on the greened gold handle and the door gave and I stepped into the brown, aging darkness of a small gold lobby with wine-colored carpeting on the floor. There was a brown plank-veneer snack bar along the far wall. There was a yellowed, cut-glass chandelier hanging from the ceiling in the center of the lobby. Against the wall behind the snack bar there was a disused punch mixer, the kind that has a transparent rectangular drum in which the drink is constantly spraying against the sides. There was drab homey furniture in the lobby that looked like it had never been used. There were faded oils on the walls with pictures of people who didn't have any faces. The lobby had the anonymous, misbegotten homeliness of mortuaries and brothels.

Faint music sounded from somewhere: the cheesy pulse of still-living disco beyond the quilted brown vinyl double doors. I pushed through them and went in. I heard the music louder now, the sound of muffled conversation. I walked slowly down the carpeted runway, stopped about a third of the way down and stood waiting for my eyes to grow used to the dark.

The theater was all gray. The seats, curtain, people. They had torn out some of the seats and put in round tables and stools on a level parquetry floor. A bar had been built into one of the walls and behind it a barman was wiping glasses under a red neon martini glass tipping continually in successive frames to the right. The barman was a paunchy, balding man with the look of a vaudeville wrestler, with loose blue skin that had been shaved the day before. He had a red, drink-molested, politician's nose. He had striped suspenders and a tank undershirt, a polka-dot shoestring bow tie. A few thin strands of gray hair were pasted like a garnish over his shiny domed head. His skin was pale and he had the quality of invisible eyes so that even when he was looking at you he wasn't looking at you and you were not looking at him.

I went and sat down by a green lamp at the end of the bar and the bartender's eyes flicked to me, up from the yellow, crumpled comic he was reading. He blinked and squinted and operated a dead cigar through the blue push-doors of his mouth. At his elbow there was a light velvet drink, the maraschino cherry glowing incandescent like a bulb, illuminating the cold liquor with a nightmare underwater clarity.

He took the cigar out of his mouth, licked his lips and pursed them together. He made expressions like he was trying to arrange his eyebrows without touching his face. "We ain't open for another couple hours yet, pal," he said, trying the phrase for sound. And as he spoke the stubble of his mustache seemed to reticulate and arrange like filings in a magnetic field.

I blew a cloud of pale gray smoke and let it hang in the air and he measured the radius with his cigar, discovering that it corresponded to the monetary quantity 5 cents, which is the measurement from the center of a hotel lobby to a point on its exterior, or in other words exactly one-hundredth the radius of the hard-boiled universe.

I took out my wallet and showed him the deputy's badge I got out of a gum machine. "Could I get a whiskey?" I said softly, with hushed overtones of Hollywood muscle. Thick, pale fingers reached to the shelf. The bartender splashed bourbon in a glass, yellow and metallic and glittering to match the color of the badge I had shown.

"That *was* copper I seen, wasn't it, John?"

"Private copper. I only let it out on Ash Wednesdays," I said. But then he didn't seem to get the gag and come to think of it I didn't get it myself.

"You wouldn't happen to have a cigar on you, would you, Bo?" the bartender asked. I didn't have any cigars. I had a schematic of a submarine in an inner pocket of my coat. I unfolded it and spread it out for him and he examined it under a shot glass, tapping various parts.

The old fashioned stood like a jelly glass on the table: reddish bourbon and a smell of closed scrapbooks, bandaged horses, the only hospital for a hundred miles. I said, "Thanks Doc, the medicine's a ripple." Faint in pool darkness, the booze grew out of my eyes like afternoon sky.

The theater was dim all the way down to the stage, with the floating feeble smoke of lamp light, old gray curtains trailing yellow gold. The ceilings were dark and phosphorescent with a nighttime searchlight panorama and a sign that said "Hollywood."

It seemed a rehearsal was in progress, only now the music wasn't going any more. A pretty, ordinary girl stood in heels, a corset and a feather boa and there were voices somewhere down below the stage and the silhouettes of three faces that seemed to be talking amongst themselves.

I sipped at my drink, swilled it around, watched the whiskey coat the insides of the glass. I got out a cigarette. The bartender tossed a book of matches onto the bar counter: a red, striped matchbook with a heart on the cover.

Music began violently and then suddenly stopped and one of the voices said something and the girl with the green boa walked off the stage and another girl advanced tentatively toward the lights, walking in shiny, red stiletto heels. Her hair was thick and black and loose and she wore a sequined corset that was pushed up against her breasts. She wore net stockings and a red garter belt. A purple satin top hat was cocked low over her left eye. Beneath it her face was masked in thick white powder, with greased kiss curls, thickened lashes, metallic eye shadow and dark red lips. There was a penciled mole on her left cheek. Her face was motionless and remote.

She stood there beneath the colored bulbs, before the striped curtains that were reminiscent of a circus more than a burlesque show. "Okay, let's see it," a gravelly female smoker's voice said and the recorded music began again and she began to move. She seemed to turn and lean like a windup dancer, moving mechanically, with mannered, urbanely robotic movements. Her face was flat as she swung a leg over a high-backed stool that, now that it came partly into the round white spotlight, could be dimly seen at the edge of the stage. Her skirt was a crimped drapery of crimson taffeta with golden butterflies sewn in.

She danced around the small stage. She pushed one strap off her shoulder, then the other; and then she made a careless, sweeping gesture and at the end of it she didn't have any clothes on. The music went loud and she began to dance around wildly, shaking her tits, shaking her ass. She began climbing up the brass pole. I looked away then, down at the bar counter, stirred my drink. I didn't want to see.

The bartender came and leaned his lips close in my ear, breathing of stale menthol cigarettes. "*Señor bueno señorita*, unh?" he rumbled, "Swell broads they got here what I'm tryina say." I said something you better believe and he laughed at that. "Yeah, *si bueno, eh amigo?*" and he nudged me and the laugh became a gurgle that turned into a cough that cashed itself into the sink. After what seemed like a long time the music stopped and the lights stopped and the dancing stopped and the show now was over.

I got up and spread some change on the counter and tossed a few crumpled bills. I lit a cigarette, walked back up the runway to the lobby where a few girls stood around clutching clear rectangular plastic bags. I leaned against the wall and waited and smoked, the smoke hanging almost motionless on dry, stagnant air. Every now and then the ladies room door would swing out and another girl would emerge.   But not the dark-haired dancer.   A minute or two more and I crushed out my cigarette in a jar of beach sand and walked down the hallway, running my hand along the gold wallpaper.

A push door marked Fire Exit stood half open at the end of the hall with the powder-blue shadow of the alley beyond.   I walked toward it, past a bank of pay phones and slower on the right, past a half-open doorway.

There was a makeup table littered with jars and powders; a mirror bordered with cream-colored bulbs; stone gray walls.   In the mirror, as I walked slowly past, for a second I caught a glimpse of a flat white face, black hair and painted lashes; the soft pinkness of a breast.   I pushed out into the alley beyond, into the daylight again, trying to shake off the cloying, hypnotic peeper's trance.

I waited there in the alley, sheltering behind newspaper. But of course the cover story was about a guy like me.

Suddenly the green metal door angled open, darkness blurred from inside: a slender, long-legged brunette in a brown wool coat the color of coffee. She came out into the alley, brushed past me without seeing me. I folded down the paper, saw her dark hair trailing around the corner onto the street.

I ran softly, passing through shadows. I looked at my watch, watched her go down the sidewalk on the south side in the harsh, late yellow sun. My fingertips touched the rough cold bricks. The air was warm on my skin and very dry. She got into a car on the boulevard: a blue Nova with yellow primer showing on the roof.

I got to my car as she was making a U turn at the corner. I jumped in and clashed the gears and drove. I traced her through the brown streets with a couple of cars between us. She made a right on Motor and then a left onto Venice Boulevard, moving smoothly from corner to corner without slowing down. I got stuck behind a pickup truck with a fiberglass camper shell that obscured my vision. I fought to get around it. When I pulled onto Venice she was gone.

I gambled and swerved and drove across three lanes of traffic, taking a right onto Sepulveda Boulevard. I saw her car making the climb on the long grade out of Culver City. I drove fast and horns blared and I caught up with her just as she was pulling into the parking lot of the supermarket at the corner of Palms and Sepulveda, the one that used to be Market Basket and before that it was Leonard's and before that it was something else. I parked two rows behind her and slumped down in the seat, put a hat on and pulled it down low. In her rearview mirror I thought I had seen the reflection of her eyes.

I sat in the car and watched and waited. The late sun shone through the rolled-up window and threw a single crude slat of shade from the sun visor across my face. In the dryness of the air there was something cold. White planes droned slowly across the sky. Somewhere a dog barked.

After a while she came back out and walked to her car, got in and drove off. I followed her. She went back to the club. I guessed she'd only gone out for a carton of cigarettes or something. She went back in and I drove away.

* * *

I drove up into West LA and got a hot dog at a stand off Santa Monica Boulevard, across from the Police station, next to a bail bonds place. I ate in the car. The radio droned weakly and made voices in the yellow afternoon. A TV was moving through the rusted screen door of the bondsman's.

After a while I got out of the car and threw the lunch in the trash. I walked up Sawtelle Boulevard toward the VA. I walked the mile or so of road around the hospital. After that I went and sat in a show.

The show got out around ten and I came out with the flow into hot night air. I got to the car. I pulled out into the streets. I vibrated and pulsed in the traffic and dulled myself in lights.

9

It was late in the place. The marquee was dim and small men didn't stand in the doorway yelling anymore and the long yellow tongues of neon had ceased to buzz and flash and inside there was pink dusk. The night was in the home stretch now.

I walked through the vinyl push doors, under the bouncer's yellow gaze. He had black Elvis hair, big and soft-looking but strong. His legs in his purple jeans were swollen like something that had been underwater too long.

Through the room the shadows of dancing girls moved in the floating cigarette haze up by the ceiling; the mute hours of one and two. The gleaming disco ball rolled gray and broken over the walls and the small dance floor and there was a low, unfocused murmur of drink-blurred voices and the lighted jukebox softly going. The girls, some of them were on stage, going through the motions – chewing gum, dancing tiredly in high heels and cheap string bikinis, some of them were on the dance floor, edging around with paying customers to the rhythm. In the corners thin girls stood folding their arms against the air conditioning draft.

I went and threw a leg around one of the barstools, leaned my elbows on the counter. "Yeah, hiya chief," the bartender said without looking at me. I put a cigarette in my lips. His eyes were fixed on the television.

A fat businessman sat beside me at the bar. He was dressed in a rough, checkered wool blazer, his blue pale wrists protruding from the sleeves, sparsely covered with wiry black hairs. He held a shot glass between the thumbs and forefingers of his large, fleshy hands and was minutely arranging the glass on the bar counter. I turned around on the stool and stared off toward the stage.

A very young girl in a pink bathing suit came up

behind me, fading in quickly in a smell of warmth and perfume. She rested on my shoulder on small brown hands. I turned around and she looked up at me with large wet eyes. "I hab loom," she said. "You wan guflen?" And I put my arm around her, the way you do, full of fleeting, makeshift passions. A battered RCA sat on a shelf above the bar. Orange flames of brush fires waved like goldfish in the blue glass. The bartender had a glazed expression on his face like a man listening to rain.

After a while the dark-haired girl came up and leaned on the counter. I watched her out of the side of my eyes, standing there with two Coca-Cola bottles and a slip of blue paper on a tray.

She turned around and leaned on a bar stool. The bartender was talking to her as he was punching numbers up on the chrome cash register. She was nodding absently without looking up from the floor. She wore a blue silk dress with a Mandarin collar, slit high up on the side, showing a lot of sheer blue nylons and above the stocking a crescent of pale thigh.

She left the bar, went back through the smoke over to a small, round table full of sailors and glasses. They were drinking beer, whistling halfheartedly, throwing dollar bills and crumpled newspaper at the dancing girls on stage. She pushed the bill down into an orange plastic container with other blue papers inside. Smoothing her dress behind her she sat down again and she was nodding, smiling with a half-amused wistfulness that seemed to live in her eyes. Her expressions had a limp, pointless quality, like the clothes of children.

I could see her. I could see my own face, pale gold and veined in the mirrored panels behind the bar, sad like old photographs: gone flesh ebbs, the eyes see calm years. There were photographs behind the bar of old film stars. Behind my face, in the mirror, naked dancing girls convulsed on stage.

The bartender came over and I ordered house Scotch. I turned around on my barstool, leaning my back against the bar. I trailed my eyes around the room in a meandering orbit, letting them fall on her each time. Then I stared at her openly, brazenly like I was made of wax. She never once looked up, kept staring down at the carpet beside her shoe, smiling with a slight, rueful amusement like an older sister putting up with things. I thought, "She knows I'm watching her." Most people look at you from time to time, just out of restlessness; but to never look at someone? No. That was too much. My mind was racing now, very clear.

One of the sailors got up and walked over to the bar with a sheaf of blue papers like tissues between his fingers. He could be seen talking to the barman, sometimes shaking the papers in the barman's face, sometimes smacking the papers with the back of his hand.

I did some more sitting around, smoked cigarettes like

it was a job in pictures. I smoked until my heart was jumping in my chest and my hands trembled and cold beads of sweat were trickling down my temples. I sat there for what seemed like a long time, not hearing the music anymore, not seeing the people.

I ground out my cigarette and fished out another. And as I was lighting it she raised her eyes and looked at me. And a small black door opened somewhere in the back of her eyes. Something occult seemed to pass between us, imploring, familiar. She dropped and then lifted her eyes again very slowly as if they were made of lead. As this was happening it was silent in my mind.

And then the place seemed to come alive again with the light and the noise and the smoke. She took a small sip from a tiny glass of Coca-Cola and smiled wincingly at what some guy had to say. I turned away, turned back to the bar and sat looking down through the booze. Maybe she felt it too, that suspicion, that nameless aversion of kindred spirits, the bad aftertaste of sincerity. I shook my head, made an automatic gesture, put down the whisky in a swallow.

* *

Time passed; the sailors left the table, sauntering for the door like sore, tired men. The dark-haired girl walked slowly toward the counter with languid grace, with a black, cork-lined tray on her upturned hand, empty except for some change and glasses and crumpled green bills that waved in the breeze from the ceiling fan.

A gray cigarette smoldered at the side of my mouth. I finger waved to the bartender and ordered a Canadian Club. I got up and walked over to the register.

I turned toward her and leaned a stiff arm on the bar. I said, "Haven't I seen you someplace before?"

She turned her head and looked at me as if it was the first time.

I clicked a lighter and she moved her mouth to the flame, holding the cigarette carefully between two fingers. She took a drag of the smoke and blew it out. "And where was that?"

"I dunno," I said. "See, that's what's strange."

She looked at me intently for some seconds, knitting her brows, her eyes boring into mine. Then her face relaxed suddenly and she looked away. "I don't re-member." She stared into the gray air. A dead, grating silence fell between us. I looked around and could find nothing to say. What there had been between us had grown dead with contact.

After a minute I said, "Listen... you ahh... you wanna dance with me?"

"We're almost closed," she said.

"Just one dance?"

"Yeah, okay," she said tonelessly and she linked her arm through mine and let me lead her over to the small, raised floor. She walked stiffly in red heels, giving the impression she was unused to them.

The floor was quiet and empty and we were the only ones there. I went and leaned my forearm on the jukebox ornamented with slowly turning golden discs inside. I flipped through the song menu trying to find something to play. I dropped a quarter into the jukebox and it began, lightened like stirred shade come alive and the slur of drunken sound.

I went over to her and put my hands out and she put out her arms. I took her left hand in mine. My right hand rested on the tightened fabric at her hips. Her eyes were black and vague and looked past my face at other things. And we were dancing, shuffling around, holding each other like dolls.

Every so often the music would stop and she would stand motionless and I would go and put more quarters in the jukebox and then we'd dance some more. We said nothing. We had nothing between us at the level of words.

After a while I muttered, "I don't know what's going on between us."

"What?" she said in my ear.

I said, "I mean, I guess what I'm trying to say... is it all over after this or... will you come with me tonight?"

She turned her face and it was shallowly illuminated with a clean, gray smoothness. I turned, slowly; and I could see it reflected in her face: the glimmer in me.

She said, "I'm not that kind."

I looked into her eyes, brought up my hand and traced her cheek with the backs of my fingers. And it was like I was touching something long ago. Then I said, "Listen... I'm not asking you to sleep with me. I just want to look at you... for a while. I just want to look at your face."

"Why?" Her eyes had a trace of uneasiness now, with a creeping mistrust coming into them like a slow, dawning fear. Like a memory stirring beneath the surface.

I said, "I dunno... maybe I could... photograph you? I used to... Could we maybe go somewhere and get a drink? Maybe I could explain."

"Where would we go? The bars are all closed. Anyway, I don't think..."

Suddenly I became desperate. I took her by the shoulders, held her at arm's length. I said, "C'mon, don't you remember? I've known you somewhere!"

She drew away from me very suddenly and the bouncer came from out of nowhere, moving very fast for a man his size, relaxed and steady on his feet. This wasn't cut-rate biker muscle. I could see that now.

"This guy bothering you?"

"No, listen, I... Look, take it easy, pal..." I brought out a wad of crumpled bills from my breast pocket, stuffed it into his coat, arranged it like a display. Then I took a swing at him. I had vague impressions as he carried me from the room. He was saying something. But my mind was somewhere else. His words had the droning, vivid irrelevance of a bedtime story, as sleep comes at the moment you begin to participate in the dream and everything whirls and begins to change...

I landed in the gutter, in the alley cat smell of urine and the clatter of cans. A fire hydrant knocked the wind out of me and I took the count.

And as I lay there, the dark-haired girl, pale-faced and nervously contrite in long-heeled shoes, appeared. She helped me to a sitting position, made a show of dusting me off.

"You okay?"

I straightened my tie, put a broken cigarette in my lips. I had a cut on my forehead and it was slowly, sluggishly bleeding with dark, glassy blood. "Yeah, baby. I feel like a million." She licked her white handkerchief, touched it to the skin and I was thinking, with a brush upon the blood, that I had been long ashore.

10

It was a tall green room with paneled walls, with rows of blue leather booths down one wall and down the other a long bar of dark polished hardwood. A thin, bright rectangle of yellow sunlight shone down along the bar, catching the gesture of weak smoke that rose from one of the green glass ashtrays.

We had walked along the esplanade. The yellow-white

sun glittered in raw light and there were small colored triangles moving slowly out at sea. An orange haze hung over the ocean and the water was smooth and slow like oil.

She wore a sleeveless dress of rough-woven red cotton with a square neck, embroidered with a pattern of flowers in yellow and blue thread.

It had been a spell of beach weather and the sun had burnt her shoulders dark and there was fresh, pink skin on the flat of her nose and sweat matted on her forehead in the fine hairs. She had a peculiar smell. The organic smell of perfume that a woman has worn for some time. Her hair was drawn back in a ponytail, bobbing dark against the sky.

We walked down the stone steps and over the footbridge, across the highway, onto the vast beach dotted with yellow oil drums belted with Coppertone ads. We walked by the water's edge. She looked at me and her face was entirely dark against the sun. I can't remember the way she looked. I can never remember faces.

We went into the bar and walked past the mirrored cigarette machine and the Ladies and Gents rooms with silhouettes on the smoked glass doors. She brushed past me and sat down in one of the blue leather booths lining the south wall. And I remembered again the way she moved.

The walls were turning a dim mustard color in the late

sun. The booths were backed with high partitions of dark, heavy wood that had been carved in intricate designs of brambles and flowers. Between us there was a narrow table of red Formica. There was terse blue carpet on the floor. In a corner, warming up for happy hour, a spindly man in a white dinner jacket sat at an upright piano with a fizzing highball on the ledge, picking fitfully at chords. "Me... Me... Melancholy Baby..." he sang, as if trying to find the right approach.

"I didn't know if you would come," I said. She had been half an hour late and I had waited for her in the plaster shop on the pier, turning over dusty casts of mermaids and birds.

And now we sat with nothing to say, with only the impression of a vague, telepathic intimacy as at times she looked at me, intense and troubled, resting her hand against her cheek with something turning and almost coming to in her eyes. A woman's gaze is like a handwriting. It was later that I came to read, to see that what I had taken for complicity, understanding was something else. Her hair was thick and loose, parted in the middle, black. It hung down over the sides of her face.

"No? It's where you said you would be." She picked a shred of tobacco from her lip, spoke a little too loudly. I hadn't expected to see her. "Yes, okay, three thirty; on the pier," she had told me. She acceded easily but had no ideas.

After a while I said, "So you're a dancer? Is that what you want to do?"

"It's what I am doing."

"Yeah, well I just meant... You know it's not like..."

She looked at me. She opened her mouth as if she was about to say something and then shut it again. She picked a long drink menu from its wire holder and pretended to study it intently, bowing her head down toward the table. She looked down into her lap and fidgeted with the white cloth napkin, twisting it tightly around her finger. She seemed to be talking to herself, moving her mouth very slightly, rocking back and forth.

After a minute I said, "So... do you study ballet or something like that?"

"I used to. For a long time."

"You don't anymore?"

"No."

"But you're still dancing."

"I'm doing what I have to do."

"You mean to pay the bills?"

"I guess you could say that."

"What do you mean?"

"When I stop dancing I begin to feel ill and strange thoughts come into my mind." She took a new pack of cigarettes from her bag and tore away the wrapper, packed the cigarettes against her palm, opened the box and tore out the silver paper. "I'm doing the only thing that can be done."

It was then I noticed that she was in constant subtle motion, like someone keeping time to music only they can hear.

She took out a cigarette between her fingernails and I reached over and lit it for her. The hand that held the cigarette was rather small and looked somehow withered. Maybe it was the peeling red skin on the pads of her fingers.

* *

"So you are a photographer?" she said.

"Not exactly. But I use pictures in my work."

The lights had come on in the bar and glowed feebly in the still daylit room. A short, Hispanic busboy came up and swept dirty rags over the tabletop, laid down a clean ashtray in place of the old one as if it was a magic trick. He went away again.

I puffed on a cigarette and blew tumbling smoke into the air that boiled in yellow chinks of sunlight through the ornamental wood. She rested her elbows on the table and cradled her chin in her hands. She looked at me.

"What work?"

The bartender came over in a white coat and laid down napkins.

"Detective work.   I get this... feeling at times. Something very old that I see for maybe a second.   I figure if I could get ahold of it, try to... capture it..."

"And you want to put me in your pictures?" She looked away, up at a corner of the room as though something was there.   She laughed softly, with an ease that surprised me.   She said, "I'm afraid I've lost my faith in pictures, somewhere along the way."

* *

The daylight had gone completely from the room and the lights glowed stronger in the green glass bowls. The place was quiet with the lull of early evening, when the traffic is slow and the first unnatural faces of the regulars can be seen leaning in the yellow light. "What is Niagara Falls," said a lady on the TV and the game show made a noise like rayguns.   Yellow-gray smoke threshed slowly in the blades of the ceiling fan.

We had a few drinks and tried to make small talk.   She told me she never went to see movies anymore.

She said she used to enjoy the shows, especially love stories, but recently the big pictures seemed always overpowering and she felt dizzy and nervous.

"Sometimes I read but it's hard to read. I can't remember things like I used to. I'm afraid I'm changed," she said.

11

I jiggled the key and pushed the door in. I walked around
flicking on light in the room. I opened a window to
freshen the air. The air outside was just as stale. When I
turned around she was standing at the bookcase.

She held a framed photo in her hands, looking at it, at
the people in it, the dark-haired woman, the guy with the
crew haircut, blue shirt sleeves, with the thick, hairy arms

and American smile, squinting into the sun. He held the woman around her waspish waist and she was smiling in a striped polyester sun dress that was purple and brown, an orange plastic band in her hair. In the background there was green, close-cropped grass, some cypress trees, a cinder block wall, washed-out Polaroid-blue sky.

"Your family?"

"Yeah... an old picture," I said.

She went and sat by the algaed fish tank. The yellowed grasses fingered slowly in the current. She put a hand against the side of the tank. Her black hair shone and seemed to shift softly. Her face reflected dimly in the glass.

I went and stood over her, scattered a pinch of flake food over the surface and she watched it wavering down. After a while she looked up at me. "Where are your pictures?" she said.

She held the photos in her palms by the rough curling edges. They were black and white pictures. She looked at all of them. She ran her fingers over the surface of the paper, held it obliquely to the light and looked at the glint of the grain. When she had put the last one down she asked me if I had anything to drink.

I went into the kitchen and got some glasses and heard her say yes she would pose for me, so long as she could set her own hours and she didn't have to do any nudes.

I brought out a bottle, a bucket of ice, glasses, a pewter ashtray in the form of a horse gazing into a lake. She looked at me and said, "I can't stay long."

"Okay."

I poured two drinks. We sat down. She smoked and watched her cigarette burn like an hourglass. And soon it was time to leave.

* * *

That night and all those nights I took her home blend in my thoughts. The radio was playing or maybe it was off. She watched the window, the intersections and the bright gas stations breathing gray against the glass. She picked a cigarette from the soft pack I had clipped to the sun visor and I pushed the coil lighter in and held it for her and she took it out of my hand and by that time it had gone dark and cold. Downtown looked like a cathedral this time of night.

I turned off the freeway into streets and alleys and large, bleak buildings that were just space. There were gated pawn shops, EZ credit jewelers, electronics stores that blared Mariachi music in the daytime with whirling disco lights.

I pulled up at the curb in front of an old white

building with a metal fire escape, with broken, gated windows, with a green neon sign on the rooftop that said, "Hotel." I said, "So this is the place?" She said it was nice enough.

There was a small lobby floored in checkered linoleum and a blue TV that dilated and contracted and a small gray night man that sat in there with no face.

Plastic bags and papers moved in the gutters and along the sidewalk. I said did she want me to walk her in and she said it would be all right. She started to go and then hurriedly I leaned over and put my arm around her. I pulled her close. She let me kiss her, her lips soft, dry and yielding, her eyes flat and opaque. Where I had kissed her the color had come away from her mouth.

"Is that what you want?" she said, looking at me from the far side of the car. She wasn't angry. Her face wore a resigned expression. Behind her, in the shadow of the building, a man slept, brushing the sidewalk with his woolly hair.

"No, listen..." I muttered, taking her hand and putting my fingers to her lips, trying to stop her words. She fiddled convulsively with the door handle, gave up and looked at me with a mixture of submission and contempt. I reached over her and opened the door, lunged at it and it swung open.

"Goodnight," she said and got out of the car.

"Goodnight," I said as the door slammed and she

walked quickly away and didn't look back.

She went into the glassed-in lobby and I kept watching till the doorway and the lobby and the elevator were empty again and so was I. I was the guy with his shoes on the wrong feet who looks around like it's funny. Yeah, "Goodnight." I pulled away from the curb.

"Is that what you want?" Her words came back to me as I drove through the streets, reverberating. I don't know what I wanted, exactly. Not sex; or a sex of some kind but not the sex of the flesh. Not sex; though perhaps I might mime it, through the night to lay some claim. But I had lost those wings. I didn't desire in that way any more. A woman's sex seemed excessive to me now, as did any thought of proximity. I didn't want the eclipse of women. And yet still this longing when they're not around.

I drove on home in the forensic bloom of boulevards and alleys. In the hills houses flickered as though they had blue flames inside. Not flames but some kind of glimmering, to hold them there. And me outside. With the long leave-taking. The soil of doorways, the great tunnel between rooms.

* * *

I got in around one, the soul of the wind so shiftless and

turning, wending its way, ruined with so many things: car engines and poisoned laughter, the dry, chambered, hysterical city. It had nothing to do with me. I emptied the ashtrays and rinsed the glasses. I didn't want love, the shadow, the mercy that come at times in the night. No one ever does. I couldn't watch it all down again. Down in me. I had nothing left but love, you understand, like a picture in my wallet. And if that was to go? Thought tonight I had the writing fever. I looked at the page. It was nothing but words.

I drank and after a while the thought of her drifted. I turned on the smoke and let it dissolve, lay back blowing rings in other rooms. Maybe the touch of satin fingers somewhere in this world. Somewhere. Yeah, sure. So trumpet the mute voices, throng the ring with impossible ladies. They come out of the corners with newspaper mugs, faces like all the crowds of men. Somewhere in all those roses it was late.

I sat there for a while drinking, smoking, listening to the music and getting pretty loaded. It didn't make me feel any better but at least it made me feel different. I got so tired of living in this same small box.

12

I pushed the dash lighter in and put a cigarette to my lips with cold, brittle fingers. The car rounded the top of one of the long curves that thread between the rough-hewn brown California hills. There was broken wood and wire fence, an expanse of rubble and field. A sign with a bell under it read, El Camino Real.

"Click." I lit the cigarette, the sound lingering in my head like an echo of my thoughts, as though my thoughts had gone outside and

wandered around. Maybe because I had so little desire to get where I was going, my memory was very sensitive and each sound or vision seemed to touch off separate long ideas. Like some kind of inventor I found my memories rushing around me with the speed. What is it about travel that brings up the past? Maybe it's the road's yawning gray mesmerism that mixes up the time. I close my eyes and distant scenes rush my thoughts.

"Ago." It had been a long time now, or so it seemed. Time that went so fast, burned so clean leaving hardly a trace. Was I older now? Already my youth was a swirling long illusion that passed like a drunken night and left few details.

She sat by the window in the armchair I had put there, beneath the yellow light of the standing lamp. She chain-smoked restlessly, turning through the glossy pages of a magazine. On her fingernails there was chipped black lacquer.

December had come and the streets were bleached cold with the hard, white winter and the season had turned in the drugstores and the vacant lots that were now full of straw and Christmas trees instead of straw and pumpkins and the still, blind sun had gone dark by five o'clock, casting long metallic shadows over Wilshire Boulevard. Winter had come and summer had slipped away, so slowly you hardly thought it was going. I had arranged a vase of flowers on a circular, black end table beside her. I adjusted the tripod and screwed the camera down.

It was an old plate camera with a cloth hood and a bellows focus made of cracked maroon leather. I'd got it in a pawn shop on Western Avenue, traded a TV that never worked. I was shooting slow black-and-white film without a flash and the pictures would be time exposures. As I adjusted the camera I saw out of focus that she was making odd, halting motions, like a person rehearsing a dramatic gesture or deciding on an approach.

She had arrived after ten and I had seen her from the window. Her face glowed orange in the light of the hall. Her features were smooth and weightless. She would have been dancing all the night before, spent the morning at the beach, lying on the sand.

I opened the door and she came in and walked toward the dim reflection of herself in the sliding glass door to the balcony. She put her hands against the glass, looked out over the dark town. She turned around and asked me if she could have some water.

I fetched a glass and filled it at the tap and gave it to her and she drank it and then sat down. She shook her hair loose, gathered it in her hands. From the closet I took the white dress she would wear and gave it to her. She went out of the room to put it on.

When she emerged she had washed her face. She took powder from her bag and began to apply it. I went and stood behind the camera.

She arranged herself in the chair, lit a cigarette. Her hand rested on the battered, curling wooden arm. She smiled slightly and pursed her lips and looked into the lens. A shadow of apprehension flickered in her face.

I shrouded my head in the heavy brown cloth, adjusted the focus of the glowing image projected on the plate of ground glass. Her face was pale. With the whiteness of the dress she seemed transparent, as though when I removed the focusing glass and replaced it with a photographic plate, her image would not remain in the darkened space.

I took several pictures, tripping the shutter with a remote trigger. She held still with a resigned expression as the film exposed. She said, "I didn't realize it would take so long."

"In the nineteenth century people had to sit for a long time to have their pictures taken." Between shots she turned through the pages of a book she had picked off the shelf.

She looked at it and then with a cough she said she liked the motion you see in photographs. She turned the book to show me and there were slim dancers with figures like bottles and hollow, organic forms. "It says here some people won't let themselves be photographed. They think the pictures steal your soul." Her eyes were round, dark and vacant like the eyes of a Spanish woman.

I moved her over to the wall by the kitchen. She leaned her shoulder and her head against the wall and looked at the floor with a downcast, tired expression. The light shone from behind her. I had pushed the fabric of her dress down off her shoulders and her hair was done up with ribbon and flowed in a loose ponytail that caught the light, showing the thick black strands of her hair. I asked her to turn her head, reached out with my forefinger to lift her chin. She was tense to the touch and resisted my movement. I drew my hand away.

"You want to have music? I'll play some music." I switched on the radio and it came on with a blurting sound and I tuned it and a monotonous falsetto continued through the grille. White Christmas. I opened the shutter and she was still.

I took another photo and her eyes were murky with a look of soft confusion, as though someone had spoken at her ear and she did not understand.

I took another picture: she was lying with her hair splayed over the couch behind her, her mouth slightly open, her eyes rolled upward. The black of her eyes seemed to bleed and flow into her hair. The light shone on her shoulder and on her powdered cheek.

After a while she seemed to become restless. I had posed her with a round hand mirror and her hair done up. I photographed her from behind, telling her to move the mirror until I could catch a fragment of her face. Her other hand was touching at her hair and around her shoulders I had draped a loose, dark robe. She began to fidget and seemed to fight to keep still. And when I was beginning to wonder uneasily if she would tell me soon that it was time for her to leave, she cleared her throat softly and said, "I don't like the idea of photographs... like you could hurt me somehow."

I felt a sudden tightness in my stomach. A coldness at the back of my neck. "What makes you say that?"

"I don't know. Maybe there was something that happened in the past."

"Did somebody hurt you?"

"I don't remember. It was a long time ago."

I reached out and put my hand on her shoulder. I said, "You could talk to me. Please. I think it's important."

"I don't remember," she said quickly and shrugged my hand away. And then, after a pause, more quietly, "How do you make the pictures?" She turned around and looked at me.

I sat down, let out my breath. "You, ahh... you shine light through the negative onto sensitive paper."

"What are the pictures made of?"

"Silver, mostly. The light rusts the silver and it turns into the dark places."

13

Nights after she had gone I'd work in the darkroom, sift the gray pictures in the trays.

As the image developed, my mind began to drift out of focus. My head began to nod. White smoke of lamplight; pale skin; folded arms and coal black hair; murky, apprehensive eyes. There was something, something in her picture that I couldn't find in moving life. I stared at it, droning in and out of consciousness

Suddenly and yet gradually like a tolling bell the time went away and now at last I seemed to remember, though the words were written in closed drawers.

I was going back, far back. Into the past. A reverberating era that moved behind my eyes, jittering in Super 8 on the living room wall.

The orange blood of childhood, the bright, wide parking lots. The trees were green and naive as Technicolor. I could remember films. I could remember my mother smiling in her pleated dress, her dark hair. She was waving, saying something with the bleached floating candor of home movies, mouthing words through her smile and then...

Where was I now? There was something. A different life that lay beneath these images like a tape that hadn't been completely erased. That you could hear faint and confused. No pictures but something. The feel of pictures. The feel of words.

"When you left..."; "the one I... "; pale, pink coldness; luminous slumber; sunlight breaking in a chamber briefly; "...she just run, on the running..."; a confusion of voices; a face in the glass; pale flowers; dark hair.

Slowly I came back to where I was, opened my eyes. What was it now? Faint pictures still breathing. I didn't know. I couldn't remember. Obscurely I knew that I had done something. Something very bad. I had a feeling as if all the pieces of my life suddenly fit into place – the loneliness, the deadness, all the long time. It all made sense to me now, for a moment. In this memory of crime. What had I done? I couldn't feel it. It was taken away from me like an anaesthetized limb, white and misshapen, while I slept.

14

It was starting to get cold. A rain had passed. The sky was clear and deep purple and it seemed the same color as her hair as she stood at the window in a thin yellow cotton dress. The moon hung in the sky like a white stone.

She spent a long time at the window. She spoke to herself in a voice I couldn't make out. After a while she turned back into the room.

She walked toward me, running a finger along the edge of a bookshelf as if she was testing for dust. Looking at the shelf in the dim light she said, "Can I stay with you tonight?"

I sat in the easy-chair in the shadow of the room. My hand glowed with the cigarette I was smoking. I said, "Yes." I asked her why and she said she was afraid. She was afraid of sleep and fitful, violent dreams. She asked for a drink and I went into the kitchen and made some highballs.

She lay on the couch staring up at the ceiling, smoking, watching the smoke trail up on the draft. She said, "Lately I've been having strange thoughts.

"Do you believe in signs and omens?

"Yesterday afternoon I was looking out of a window. A flock of crows flew into the sky over the buildings. They flew into the sky and it was like I knew they would, after I saw them. And as I watched them fly away a very peculiar feeling crept into me. It was quiet, close, warm and very familiar. But not pleasant. It was like a slow nightmare. It was like the birds were touching a disease inside me, opening a door. And suddenly I felt sick deep inside. Like something had reversed in me. Suddenly I knew what it was to be damned."

She rose and put her feet down on the floor and sat for a while, staring into the half-distance; then shook herself and smiled slightly. She took another swallow of drink and crushed out her cigarette. Her hand moved whitely in the shade. "I have to dance so much," she said, "to purify myself. The days are getting so short now."

15

It was three o'clock and I was sitting in my office. I'd been in there for days, looking at pictures on the walls, clicking over and over through the carousel.

Sunlight glinted through the slats of the drawn venetian blinds at the window. There was muted, disjointed sound in the street below. In the building there were the sounds of men.

I went through the pictures over and over, looking for something. And as I looked I began to feel as though there was something continually forming just out of my field of view.

I pulled a long, green bottle from the deep desk drawer. I poured myself out a drink and drank it, poured out another and I drank that too. I killed the bottle. And as I settled into the deep lush quiet I thought back to when I was something different. When I was someone else. I slumped in the chair.

I sat there for a long time, unmoving. And when I closed my eyes I had images that flashed on me with terrific sudden vividness, too fast to see, like things seen out of the window of a speeding train. Then, gradually, the images slowed down. And then I realized it was the same image, over and over. The image was a rectangular hole cut very sharply into dark, wet earth. In the hole there was a pale woman with black hair. Her eyes were open. It was raining. Silver flecks of rain pattered around her red lips.

16

The smell of the booze hit you in the face along with the cigarettes and the music. I hadn't seen her in several weeks. The last few nights merged in my thoughts in a montage sequence of flashing lights and whirling disco globes; impassive waitresses drifted on platform spaghetti-strap sandals, with trays on one shoulder and eyes that had seen enough.

reflection near the stem.

Suddenly I had a bad taste in my mouth. "You should be careful with that," I said.

"Too late, it's my third tonight!" she said brightly in a sing-song voice and laughed. First just a little and then as if something was very funny, rocking back and forth and smacking her palm against the table, her eyes flashing with a sudden hungry vivacity. She seemed a different person.

She rattled another cigarette out of the soft pack lying loosely on the table. She drew it in her mouth, took a drag and her face wrinkled in revulsion.

"Uhhhf! You want this?" she said through the smoke, "It tastes like metal. Oh my neck is... so... cramped." She kneaded the muscles with her hand. "Have you been here long?"

"No."

"God the fucking *music* ! I swear it's been like two solid hours of house! How can you dance to that? Hunh? You have to be a complete fucking *moron*. I mean it's just thump, thump, thump, thump!" She pounded her fist on the table. "I mean there's nothing, there's just nothing, nothing, NOTHING... I dunno, don't mind me I'm just flipping out Jesus Christ this guy gave me a few puffs of a joint a few hours ago? – maybe an hour ago? – and *fuck* it's like the bottom dropped out of my *mind* or something I already took the acid and that hadn't really come on at all but right after I smoked that joint – only two puffs! – *really* weird feeling like everything was just... I dunno you think it was laced? I've been..."

The music changed and the room was suddenly full of clanking, the thud of a tambour and chanting, droning, circling and then the groove exploded in hard trance music. She jumped up, shouting, "Oh I love this! Why aren't you dancing? Come on, get up! Dance with me!"

She took me by the wrist and ran down the stairs, dragging me after her onto the floor. She drew me into the middle of the room. She began to dance. She was not looking at me. Not looking at anything. Her mouth was open. Her eyes were glassy. A kind of vacant fanaticism came over her and she was smiling and shaking her head, shuckling her hand like she was rattling dice, her tongue lolling about her lips. There was something uncanny in her eyes.

Her body was like water as she danced. The specks of the mirror ball floated over her. Her arms floated out over her head and we were very close, pushed together in the thick, heaving, promiscuous crowd.

It was getting very hot and her mouth was open and her eyes were black in the orange light. Her face was light with ease. It was the face of a very young girl.

She was smiling and laughing and she was yelling in my face. At first I couldn't hear what she said. Then I realized she was speaking in a language I'd never heard. There were white flecks of spittle at the corners of her mouth. She was shaking her arms, shaking her head, her eyes rolling upward. She was going into a trance.

17

As the days went by I saw her less and less. Until she did not come around at all. And then, unexpectedly, one night in December, sometime after midnight she knocked on my door.

She came in and was very drunk and told me so. She spoke loudly and twirled in the center of the room and almost fell, clutching at the arm of a chair.

She moved to the gilt-framed, oval mirror over the built-in shelves. She stood unsteadily, looking in the glass. She touched at her hair. Suddenly she turned violently away.

She moved along the wall, disturbing the pictures with thin, white fingers, singing. I asked her could I get her anything and she said thickly, "Whiskey."

"Drink some water first," I said and she waved an arm and walked a little and sank into the chair.

I brought over the ottoman and she put her feet up, splayed out her hand in a dramatic gesture and called my name.

"Johnny," she said, saying it aloud as though just to hear the sound of it. She went on saying it, over and over until it was only sound. Then she began to make rhymes by substituting all the letters of the alphabet for the J and she mumbled those with varied intonations. I brought her a glass of water and she pushed it away and shivered as her fingers came in contact with the glass. She needed whiskey, she said. If I wouldn't give it to her then she'd go somewhere else. She'd take some pills, she said.

I went back to the kitchen and brought out a bottle and glasses and stood for a moment in the doorway watching her and she did not see me. I realized I had become used to her absence; and now her presence seemed foreign. She seemed smaller, paler. With hectic effort she got out a cigarette and lit it and the smoke trailed away. Her cigarette hand fell limp at her side. Her shoulders seemed thin and frail beneath the fabric of her dress.

I walked over and set the glasses on the end table, poured some liquor in each. I picked up her glass and put it in her hand and she clicked it against her teeth and drank it down and had me pour her another. I gave her some more, set the bottle down.

She began talking very softly, in the dreamy, half-there way of extreme drunkenness. She told me about her childhood and how she lived in the far north and each day she would walk several miles in the snow. She said she was always afraid she would lose her way, and the trees and the mountains would all become turned around. She spoke on in a high, sick whisper, looking down at the floor.

"I guess I feel that way now, like I've lost my way. I thought I knew where I was going. They say time is a healer but I don't know. It seems there's a little less each day."

* * *

After a while she drifted off into a deep, drugged sleep and her chest rose and fell with her breathing. I brought a comforter out of the hall closet and lay her on the sofa and lay the comforter over her and left the light on and went to sleep in the chair. I watched her sleep. And at times her eyes twitched and I thought she might be dreaming. She was close to me and far away. I lay back in the chair and looked at the ceiling and soon I slept.

I awoke somewhere in the cold, early hours. My tie and my jacket stirred slowly together in my remembering vision, with the gaudy colors of a mixed drink. The room came into focus: the books, the lamp, the telephone, the long private space. Outside the rain came down in a gray hail and there was the iron smell of clouds.

I shifted gently, stiffly in the long divan, felt the rough, olive wool rasp against my knee. I turned and began to massage my arm, rubbing back the circulation. I saw her then, lying on the sofa and I had forgotten she was there.

I had a brief sensation of coldness – an expression in her eyes, a pale, hollow atmosphere. It flickered and then went away. I realized I had no feeling, seeing her. Sleep distills things. Thoughts come quietly with a certain inevitability and one can accept ideas that would otherwise be intolerable: a parting; a change in the weather. And yet there seemed something unnatural in this. How could it be that this girl so near to me now would be removed and estranged in time? It seemed illogical, like all separations. But I knew then, with a kind of dream intuition, that she would pass from my life. Soon I would not see her any more.

It was near morning and she lay straight under the bedding I had brought her, her face blank and clear like a sleeper's; but her eyes were open and cold, staring up at the ceiling in the faint light.

"I can't sleep," she said. "I don't seem to sleep much any more. I take... pills. I never sleep in the night but toward morning they give me rest and strange, gentle dreams. I don't know what it is with me. I think I need to rest." We were silent then, for a long time. It was cold in the room. Once or twice I looked to the window, thinking the sky had begun to pale.

18

It was like this for a while. She would show up in the late night, very drunk. She would come in and sit in the middle of the couch and talk to me earnestly while I made some drinks. I sat in the easy chair.

She never asked to see the pictures I had taken. When I mentioned them she avoided the subject and smoked more rapidly, speaking fitfully.

She told me she had quit her job at the club. Soon, she said, she would not need anything. "I will disintegrate into pure motion. Motion is the only thing that keeps me alive." As she spoke she rocked back and forth with her arms held tight against her sides.

I said, "I think maybe you should see a doctor."

She shot a suspicious glance at me. "A doctor? No. No doctors. I'll be fine. Just need to keep moving is all. Soon I'll be free."

I said I didn't like the sound of that and she said I didn't understand.

"It's not a bad thing. It'll be beautiful. It's just frightening sometimes, the change."

I said, "I don't know what that means."

* * *

She would stay until dawn and then, as the sky was beginning to lighten, she would gather her things, hanging for a moment and wavering in the doorway and then leaving very quietly so as not to wake me if I slept on the couch. It was as though she was released from something with the morning; and company, which meant so much through the night, began to fade.

I would hear the knob rattle and the lock catch and I would open my eyes to blue, living darkness; and I would wonder what time it could be. It was silent in the room and the furniture glowed with a muted phosphorescence and seemed draped in cloth. I could see very little and this might still be a dream, surfacing but not yet pricking the skin of sleep.

And then the evening would come back into my head, with the alcohol and the cigarettes, and I would know it must be dawn. She left with the night, taking the darkness away in her skirts.

19

"I don't remember," she said.

"You must remember something."

"I don't think about it."   And she looked at me, steadily; then she looked away, down at the table, down at her hands and the small, red, withered fingers. Her hair was parted down the middle of her scalp and fell in loose, thick braids around her shoulders.   Her eyes were indolent, empty and black in her pale wax-colored face.

She held a half-dead cigarette loosely in her fingers. The ends of her braids were tied with bits of orange string.

I leaned back against the brown, quilted vinyl of the booth, looked off down the aisle at the old white waitress; the shiny linoleum floors; dark, reflecting windows; the stark Polynesian counter. At the light, on Overland, a green Culver City bus idled.

"It's a dark night," she said, leaning against the window glass. "You know how sometimes the lights reflect from the clouds. Then the city seems closer. You can't see the sky. You don't feel so alone."

"I'm sorry you feel that way," I said.

"Oh well, I..." She looked back and saw my face. "...I'm sorry. I guess I shouldn't say..."

The waitress came along with the coffee pot, poured weak coffee into the cups. She gave us a weary, disgusted look as she was pouring it, as if she was falling for an old trick: "I pour the coffee and you people drink it. Then I gotta pour it again." She went away and I put some cream in my coffee and stirred it around. The spoon clinked dully on the porcelain. There were purple lipstick stains on the rim.

"You see..." She looked at me, past me. Her eyes were heavy and remote. She looked like she was thinking of something that had happened long ago.

"...See, I'm exactly the same as everyone else, except... different." She focused on me and something clutched in her eyes, a shadow swept across her face. She went on, speaking very precisely, patting the tabletop as she spoke as though setting things straight.

"I think there must have been some... accident... when I was conceived. I've given a lot of thought to it. There must have been some... hypocrisy, some malpractice, some shady business.

"...Oh I suppose it has to be that way." The words came out in a rush, as though for the benefit of some third party, standing in the shadows, easily offended. "I'm not complaining, you understand.   It's just that I was... molded... imperfectly. In my spirit. In my heart." She smiled briefly, tightly. "Too many cracks."

"If only it wasn't... " She looked around furtively and then bent her head low. She spoke quietly, through gritted teeth. "If only it wasn't for the night. I never sleep in the night anymore. He comes in. Anxiety is the worst part of madness."

* *

She struck her head against her hand like a bather trying to remove the sea. She grinned slowly, closing her eyes, showing me small, white teeth. She was moving her head, swaying gently with her eyes closed. "Oh Johnny, I'm still tripping. I'm tripping every day. It's really frightening," she said; but she did not sound frightened. She said it as though it was a very good thing. "And my hands can touch the colors... blue and yellow and... it's like... they're all moving... with... every... sound."

Her face changed very suddenly and became utterly blank. She stared out the window, speaking in dead robot tones, her words misting on the glass. "This is not my hand. This is not my face. This is not..."

Suddenly she burst out laughing. "Oh God! I was supposed to be a saint!" She laughed and pounded her fist on the table, shaking the cups in their saucers, making the other diners look round. I reached a hand to calm her and just as suddenly she stopped.

She looked up at the ceiling with a beatific expression. Her cheeks were round. Her lips were slightly parted, full and red. Her eyes shone like a doll's. At times she seemed filled with rich, fleeting emotion. Her cheeks shone in the fluorescent light. And then her face went dim.

"It's all the... electricity," she said in a tone of dawning realization. She spoke in a small, high voice. "Everywhere they put the messages. You know, Johnny? Do you know what I'm saying?" She froze in horror and clapped a trembling hand to her mouth. "My thoughts are disintegrating as they leave my mind," she said matter-of-factly. Her face, reflected in the dark window, was pale and transparent. The headlights of cars shone through her cheek.

20

"I didn't see you," I said.

She stood before me in a long white dress, her black hair hanging lank and heavy and spilling over her shoulders.

"I came in the back way. I came in through the trees."

"Is there a path there?"

"No."

"I didn't see you."

"Maybe you were asleep."

"I can't sleep."

"Didn't you see me? I came to say goodbye."

I awoke in the darkness with the words still ringing in my head.

21

The car droned through the alley, lighting up gravel and scrap sheets of blue metal. I hadn't seen her in weeks and I'd gone everywhere asking. No one had seen her and I went from club to club. Now I was somewhere east of Union Station, beyond the tracks and the yards, in sprawling blocks of abandoned warehouses lit in hard yellow light that made all the metal gray.

I stopped the car in front of a rusted fence with a bright gash opened in the chain link. In the yard beyond, dim green stencils pointed the way along a wall of rusted machine parts. Somewhere in the distance I could hear muffled sound.

"I'm starting to come on," I thought. The dashboard lights were greener, the buildings were strange. For a long while I had felt a sense of hyper-normalcy: a total absence of inebriation as though the drug had welded my mind and I could never be intoxicated again. Now that seemed to have been like the dead calm that comes before a hurricane. I had a funny taste in my mouth. A strange sense of continuity like a hum you could feel but not hear. The steering wheel was hot and thick and pulpy to the touch.

I parked the car, killed the engine and the lights. I began to hear a distant throbbing. I opened the door and went out. I got out a pencil flash and played it briefly along oil drums and cans.

There were footprints on the ground and then on the walls of the building there were green spray-painted arrows. I followed them.

The arrows slanted down low on the wall, leading to a service door that had been kicked in and hung in splinters of fresh pale wood. On the gray cement above it you could see an unintelligible picture sprayed in stencil and the club name, "Bionic," in elaborate, Old English lettering underneath.

I felt my way down a poured cement staircase and down another and the sound was much louder now. It was twelve-thirty by the luminous dial of my watch.

I was going down. My head was at ground level. The windows were small and made of pebbled gray chicken-wire glass. Some of them were broken and from the darkness outside came a faint breath of cold air.

I went down another stairway and now I was underground and the air was musty with the smell of cigarettes and damp concrete. My eyes became slowly accustomed to the light and I began to see in the gloom. There was a blue patch of color down at the end of the hall.

I walked down the hall into a dim, smoke-filled room, into the draft of fans blowing cold, heavy air down on the violet floor. It was a large room, almost in darkness, with uncertain shapes of people moving slowly in front of the walls.

There was no sound of voices. The room was calm with a deep roaring rumbling from the speakers. Up in a corner the DJ worked, illuminated in a single finger of white light hanging at the end of a coil of thick wire. The DJ had a thick mass of unkempt black hair and wore a white dress shirt and black suspenders. With headphones cupped to one shoulder he rolled a wide black dial between his thumb and forefinger. He was sweating profusely. His skin had the dirty gray-brown pallor of a man who hasn't slept in days. There were large dark circles spreading from his armpits.

I saw her standing by a concrete pillar, sipping at a red plastic drinking cup, swaying barefoot in a short, white cotton dress, staring at the ground. I went over to her and put a hand on her shoulder and she looked up at me. The whites of her eyes were pale blue in the black light. Her pupils were wide and dark. She smiled, licked her lower lip with a thick purple tongue and showed me the chip of paper glowing on the tip.

On tall narrow tables around the cement pillars lamps full of blue oil burned bright and lurid with something poisonous tossing and leering in the flame. My skin was hot and dry and rubbery. I licked parched lips, running a hand over the back of my neck, repeatedly clenching my teeth. My muscles had begun to ache. My heart was racing in my chest.

I got out a cigarette and fumbled for my lighter and the flame leapt out like a snake, seething with yellow light. With a flash of panic I dropped the cigarette without lighting it, walked out the door as the first rhythm began to articulate itself from the sound of the noise.

I walked along the dark hallway, up the stairs to ground level and then up another flight, kept climbing until I reached the roof.

My heart was pounding in my chest, thudding in my

head with the sound and the image of a 1920 car. The image was superimposed on my body. I could hardly stay on my feet. Pictures exploded at the back of my eyes. I clutched the blackened pipe handrail, groped up into the raw, clean, cold night air taking ragged, shallow breaths. I staggered out into the sky.

I pressed a hand to my face, gripped my forehead and slow blue and green stains flared and died away like searchlights at the back of my eyes.

With a sense of dislocation, I crumpled to my knees and lunged forward, scrabbling at the tar paper with my hands. A small stream of spittle dropped from the side of my mouth and pooled on the ground.

But I could not puke.

I stuck my forefinger down at the back of my throat, scratched at it desperately with my nail. I reeled, retching violently, the colors erupting in stars in my eyes, in patterns that were intricate and yellow and fantastically ugly, always shifting out of my field of view.

I kept on puking, heaving till nothing was left and then heaving some more, my face flushed and bulging, my eyes rolling, the taste of acid on my gums.

Soon I would lose consciousness. I knew that. And I knew that if I did it was all over for me. I was at the edge of a high, crumbling precipice, holding on...

I pulled myself up doggedly by the drainpipe, told myself I was gonna be OK. I could feel myself starting to leave my body, starting to drain away. I looked up at the sky, the stars. The stars seemed to pour into my open mouth.

I groped to my feet and started to walk in circles around the tar-paper roof and as soon as I was walking I began to feel a little better and in my head it was all lush and verdant and rippling like a thousand trees. The atmosphere seemed to flow into me. And when I closed my eyes it was like I was doing the subtlest thing in the world. Like a fever. A childhood illness I'd forgotten all these years. That now came back to me with the strange taste, the strange thoughts. Everything was out of a movie. Everything I did was from somewhere else.

My throat was dry.

I had to get water.

I groped down the stairway toward the basement.

I went down the stairs, down another flight, another. A heavy fullness unfolded in my body, sinking down into my feet and hands.

Back in the room the music had taken hold. I went over to the dark-haired girl. She smiled and didn't say anything. She was swaying, nodding slowly, smiling, watching the shades trail from her hands.

The music was hypnotic, repetitive, mechanical. The dark-haired girl undulated slowly with the sound of it, a look of craziness starting to come into her eyes.

The DJ gazed down impassively at the knobs and dials, gripping the black metal between thumb and forefinger. The lights of the control panel reflected in his dark glasses. Smoke trailed up from the cigarette in the corner of his mouth, arcs of ash falling and shattering like frozen logs around the flicking meters.

He gazed up into the green light that had begun slowly flashing down through the fog and the smoke, bathing the floor and the people like a beacon. His lip curled in a smile of grim satisfaction.

The lights came on and the room was filled with frantic motion; sweaty long hair lashed in girls' faces; a guy next to me was sweating heavily, looking around the room with wild, cagey eyes, bearing his teeth, wringing his hands.

A cold draft came down from the vents. The air was stifling still. Girls were taking off their sweat-soaked shirts, breasts heaving in mesh running bras, gathering their skirts, pouring large blue plastic ladles of water on their legs and over their heads and then rushing back to dance.

I was standing near the wall by the juice table, drinking glass after glass of water. In front of me hopping around in circles there was a green-eyed girl wearing a wig of long transparent hair, hopping from foot to foot as she tried to take off her clothes, a look of bewilderment on her face.

Across the floor the dark-haired girl was oblivious to anything around her, thrashing around, completely lost in the driving sound. She was grinning, her eyes wide and hysterical, her long dark hair flying about her face.

The yellow lamp lights tossed and waved and danced against the pillars, throwing brief long shadows that licked like black flames. I stared into these shadows. Above the shadows the flashing green spotlight pulsed in my face. The colored glass lit up in a green of pure familiarity. The kind of green you hardly find, green like the greenest trees, pale and milky... and then somewhere behind me I heard the scream.

I turned in the direction of the sound and saw the dark-haired girl with her hands to her temples, shaking her head violently with a look of wild panic on her face as the strobe flickered over her. There were people all around, jostling her as she lost the rhythm and was shoved back and forth by the relentless frenzy of the crowd.

All in one moment I was seeing her, pushing toward her with outstretched arms. She was shaking her head back and forth, moving faster and faster, lost in the surging confusion. The white light flickered over her. I shoved people aside trying to get to her. I whirled around blindly. All I could see was the flashing light.

22

I drove north, the wipers swishing away the pelting rain, the gray sea lost beside me in the fog. I drove until the seafood joints and filling stations became dim and less and the green hills began to dominate the landscape, hung heavy with clouds. I'd spent some time before the few yellow shop windows in the last roadside town.

The grounds were dark and vague and green, drifting and rolling in big shapes and then there was gravel under my wheels and suddenly the big cream building in front of me again. Like a castle that becomes disenchanted in the visiting I was always surprised to see it there.

Here the rain had not come yet, though blue and purple clouds pressed against the trees and the buildings, pressed down around the hills. Nurses dressed in white wheeled patients from the verandah, newspapers folded like yellow blankets over their knees. Lights went on in windows that had been dark, showing the fine diamond pattern of the grate. I flicked the cigarette I was smoking and it sparked in the black soil at my feet and then hissed and was dark. I closed the black, heavy car door with a thud.

Clipboards, fluorescent lights and orderlies, the echo of tiled halls. Visiting hours. I knew the drill: the pause like a curtain in the doorway; the careful, stylized, meaningless knock; the jacked-up smile; shrill optimism. I'd got past all that now. It seemed I'd got past so many things.

Her eyes were gone and vacant, purple-lidded, wide and almost blue. And her black hair spilled in vines and wires on the pillows. She was dressed in white, like a bride of some kind.

In the night she had been restless, Sister told me — chanting, throwing the furniture, pounding her head. And that was why she was tied, swathed in wide canvas, that was why the bruises around her eyes. I could stay a little while. I could talk but she couldn't hear me.

"She left a note," Sister told me. And I knew from the bandages she'd cut her wrists again. It got so it was like a song. I knew the refrain:

"*And after the operation, when the lights went on again – the ceilings; the faces; a cup of blue ice between heaven and earth.*"

I sat down in the hard, wooden visitor's chair, laid my hat on the white enamel table. And when Sister had gone I lit a cigarette, put it to her lips and she began to smoke.

I talked and maybe she could hear me, so full already of whispers, shipwrecked on that high, ivory bed.

"I uhh... I brought you some things... The things you wanted..." *Outside a patch of blue light drifted behind the clouds.* *"...Cigarettes, some picture postcards, a bathing suit. You can have 'em when I go, I..."* *My voice shook and trailed on me and I saw clearly, perhaps for the first time, the great difference between people. I sat there for a long time and she lay staring, the dawn sadness of white lost eyes flickering in the shadows like an empty cinema.*

* * *

I left the hospital and didn't go home. I drove on the highway, down toward Zuma, parked in the sand and gravel by the side of the road.

I walked out into the water and there was so little to give away. And as I walked out into the waves and the green sea flecked with foam, I swore that I would find her. I would find her somewhere at the bottom of the ocean, and hold her cold body in my arms.

And in the aftertime, as I went under; somewhere in the black race there were visions of humanity, like a sea of pink dancing with surges of blue and green. And I dreamt...

It is very early in the village and, as in a fable, everything is quiet and naive. The cold, hollow-dark spells in the far hours as night comes to morning. And the snow falls in ash petals on the ground, dreamy around the small houses and the thatched, pointy roofs, the sleepy red lamplight and it is permanent Christmas Eve down the lanes and alleys where you can hear nothing. Nothing except for a certain low keening like wind in the hills. Or maybe it is just a whisper of the purchaser's sadness, a shadow of fin de siècle melancholy passing over the land. We have arrived at some early age, the silent land beneath. We are falling softly through gray clouds.

We are shaken slowly from our reverie by the sodden long clopping, the desultory footfalls of the postmaster's nag on the rotten beams of the old bridge over the frozen river at the edge of town.

Closer now and clapping on the stones and we can hear her snorting now and can imagine her steamy breath. Now there is a man's voice talking, the low and fitful mumbling of the solitary traveler who has got into the habit of always thinking he's alone. He's coming up now and his mare is blustering and clamping in the snow. He dismounts, wincing, runs his glove-fingered hand along her steaming sides and she is shaking her head sideways against the reins.

The old rider with the snowy beard yellow-gray from tobacco and ruddy, wind-scarred cheeks, with the clay pipe in his teeth, with the big brown bag and the heavy harness gear, with the fur-lined cap and the pint of whiskey in his boot, he seems a good man all of a sudden. And in fact a little dog runs up to him and you can see its quick breath on the air by the first watered-down grays of a winter dawn in the cold, northern countries we are in.

He seems tired and he is gritting his teeth around the pipe which has long since gone cold. Somewhere a clock sounds from the town hall: five o'clock.

A window slides open above a shop sign and the old town widow is leaning out and her hair is still in white netting. She says something and at first it is in a foreign language and then by degrees it becomes familiar and we can soon understand the old rider, who is saying, "Don't mind if I do;" and the window closes shut and in a little while the street door opens and we can see the flickering profiles thrown almost sinister on the door and portico as they talk over the waving yellow lamp flame and then go inside and we are in a very small kitchen, with a big brass kettle hanging blackened over a brick hearth where the embers are deep violet and they throw a soft somnolence over the old postman as he thumbs the tobacco down in his pipe and holds out a match with swollen red knuckles and puffs, the flame leaping down and forth, his eyes minute and twinkling in the old flame.

We know he is saying that he cannot sleep yet as the woman is pouring him hot beer. He has to go to the house at the end of the woods. He has to deliver a small blue letter which we see sticking out of his breast pocket now that he calls attention to it with a pat.

"Oh," says the crone, "now there's a funny place if you like."

"Well," the postman says, "now there's some that'll say it's a bit on the rare side but..." Here he does some vague and generous trailing in air and waves around his pipe hand. And the smoke becomes vague and generous as well.

"Well..." the old woman softens her eyes and un-bunches her mouth. "She's always been all right to me, you understand. I'm not saying a thing against her mind. It's just those... others. Well, I mean they're not like *you* I mean now *you're* a fine figure of a man but..." We get the impression that perhaps the old woman is still fishing for a husband, someone to comfort her in the long, cold nights.

She seems to get riled to gossip and she is smoothing down her skirts; but then the man unceremoniously takes a big watch out of his coat pocket. There is an embarrassed silence and the old woman touches her cheek very gently as if it were made of china and brushes at a wisp of her hair and says, "Well, off you go mister. I've got my business to attend to yet!"

And the man smiles half-sadly and he picks up his bag and we see through the black doorway that it is a pale morning now. The door closes and darkness inside the room.

The snow is driven in flocks, it's driven in sails. The quiet lays white bandages on the land.

The old rider slowly pulls on his gloves and he wraps his scarf around and the old horse is skittish or maybe just tottering with the cold and he strokes her dappled neck as she lumbers on through the streets, toward the woods and the strange trees and though there is no sound the mare now seems graceful and walking as if in time to music as they pick their way down in the snow, through the trees, into the wood.

And at length the old man smiles and his gray eyes twinkle because he sees a little dark patch and a blurred rectangle of yellow light and, though the woods are almost sugared over in snow, you can read on the painted shingle, "The Home of Rose Red," as he passes through the gate on his nag who is looking more and more like a donkey and, in fact, begins to bray.

The old rider pauses a moment before he mounts the steps. He takes the envelope from his pocket and looks at the address. As in Citizen Kane, everything has a Russian quality and the old man smiles vainly and looks up to the skies and then he takes out a cigar and puffs at it and then throws it carelessly away. The sky is heavy and dead gray with the snow that is coming down like paper, like a ticker tape parade, like the New Year, the magical acceleration, the alcohol and the brief tinsel that come with the cold turning of the time. He mounts the long staircase, knocks three times on the door.

The sound of singing now and toy instruments. The door is flung open and the old man is as if among children, patting the jovial little men on their balding heads as they boisterously lead him inside.

He is just entering the sitting room as a thin girl is descending the curving wooden stairs. He looks up at her and she is dressed in pale housewife blue, with gathered sleeves and pleated skirts. Her hair is black as ink, blacker still. The room is strangely bare and somber with dark, hard furniture and white walls that seem almost too white to look at. The girl is putting her hair up around her shoulders, smiling with full, red lips, with small, white teeth.

"Ahhh!" says the postman and he makes a sweeping gesture that has traces of gallantry and we think perhaps he is sweet on Rose Red just like the old town widow is sweet on him.

Suddenly the little men are all quiet and bustling around, grabbing leather bags and satchels out of corners, sticking little clay pipes in their mouths almost in unison, slinging their bags over their shoulders with a purposeful air and they are off.

The postman can't help smiling as he watches them go. Then, as if brought up short in his musings, he turns with a stiff, official, embarrassed movement and, half as an excuse for himself, half as a present, he holds out the envelope he has held in his hands.

The girl takes it and perhaps she is weary of the formality, perhaps she isn't as consoled as she might be but she doesn't smile and she looks at the wall and then the old postman seems to understand. He shakes his head slowly and says, "You know, miss... what they're saying in the big town... they're saying it's, it's a new world now... that's right a new world... And Thomas Edison himself is coming to town. He's gonna be driving a big, black car. And he'll be throwing wires like tinsel through the valley, till all the trees are Christmas trees and the forest is full of voices... and if you want to say something, even to someone very far away, you can whisper... and all the trees kind of join hands and a little shiver passes through 'em and... and maybe, maybe then..." He trails off now, ashamed, like he shouldn't maybe have said nothing.

He drums his fingers idly, purposefully on the back of a chair and then stares at his hand for no reason and smiles quickly and then he takes his leave.

And the dark girl sees him out and shuts the door, moving her back against it in a gesture that is one of the remnants of her womanhood. And then she goes into the kitchen and she takes a long knife and slits the envelope open.

Out falls a small, blue card and she does not read it but picks it up and takes it over to the mantle and lays it there in a small metal box.

But as she is opening the lock we can see on the card some writing and soon it becomes clearer so that we do not so much read the words as remember them after she has put the lid down.

> Rose Red, I would miss you
> Though you peopled the flitting day.